CRISS-CROSS

Criss-Cross

Alan Scholefield
writing as
Lee Jordan

Heywood Books

© Lee Jordan 1983

First published in Great Britain by
Coronet Books 1984

ISBN 1 85481 003 0

This edition published in 1989 by
Heywood Books Limited
55 Clissold Crescent
London N16 9AR

Printed in Great Britain by
Cox & Wyman Ltd, Reading

1

Jane Hemming stood at the window of her room on the twenty-second floor of the mid-town hotel and watched evening come to Manhattan. Away to her right the sun died in a welter of sulphur and smoke over Hoboken; to her left, darkness seeped across the stricken landscape of the South Bronx, then Queens, then across the East River, coming towards her like a grey tide.

Ever since her childhood in England this had been the worst time of day for her: the dying of the light. Her father had died toward evening. Dusk, the dark; death, decay. Even the words had frightened her. She remembered the lilac trees outside her bedroom window. She would watch as the light faded and the branches twisted and turned. She would imagine eyes—she never knew whether they were animal or human—watching her. Like the windows of the skyscrapers around her now.

"You're in New York," she told herself. "The door is locked. No one can get in. There's a telephone. The lobby is filled with people."

But however hard she tried, she could not forget that Walter was somewhere out there—and the terror returned. "I'll follow you," he had said. "I'll find you."

Susie, behind her, started to make up one of her long stories. Jane only half listened. It was about a red man and a blue man. Susie was sitting on one of the two queen-size beds and she had folded her scarf to give it the vague shape of a body. She sat cross-legged in front of it, talking to it as though it were human. It was a large yellow cotton square which had been Jane's. For a year, Susie had taken it everywhere and had been beside herself with anguish on the few occasions she had been parted from it. She slept with it, she walked with it, she talked to it. Early on, Jane had mentioned her concern about the child's dependence to her mother who had said: "I wouldn't worry. You used to have a kewpie doll you took everywhere with you."

"That was a doll. This is an old piece of material."

She had eventually accepted that it was necessary to Susie. Now the scarf was worn and stained and thin in parts and sometimes Susie would put a corner into her mouth and chew it. She's using it as a thumb, Jane had thought. She's insecure and it's my fault. Mine and Walter's.

As darkness came to the city, Susie's story went on. It was as though she had opened a tap in her child's mind and was allowing all the images and thoughts to pour out. The blue man and the red man, she was saying. The red man and the blue man, over and over.

"I'm going to take a shower," Jane said.

"Miss Blackstock is hungry."

So now the scarf had become Miss Blackstock. It could have been Sir Henry, or the Prince. Sometimes it was a rabbit or a hamster, sometimes Mr. Magic. It could change into anything: a child, a pet, an adult, at the whim of Susie's mind.

"What do you want to eat?"

"*Miss Blackstock* is hungry," Susie said pedantically.

There were occasions when she would speak only through the medium of the scarf, when she would hear nothing except when she was addressed through Miss Blackstock or the Prince or Sir Henry, or whoever else she had fixed on. Jane looked at her affectionately, recalling with the tremor she would probably always feel how nearly she had lost her.

"I'm sorry. What does Miss Blackstock want?"

"Miss Blackstock . . . uh . . . umm . . . Miss Blackstock wants . . ."

Jane propped up the illustrated room service menu on the scarf. "There you are, Miss Blackstock, you have a look at

6

the pictures and perhaps you and Susie can make up your great minds while I shower. Then I'm going to phone your grandmother.''

Susie looked up and smiled. She was four and small for her age, neat in her miniature jeans and scarlet, polo-necked sweater. She had large brown eyes and enviably long lashes, fine, straight, shoulder-length brown hair. Her face, in repose, was solemn, but would light up when anything amused or interested her. She's had too little amusement lately, Jane thought. I must make it up to her.

She undressed and took a shower, leaving the bathroom door open. Susie was talking again by the time she began to towel herself. The lights in the bathroom had a pinkish tone and as Jane dried herself she inspected her body in the big, square mirror as objectively as she could. Everything was in the right proportion, except that there was more of everything than she might have wished. She looked critically at her breasts. She had not had enough milk to feed Susie. ''Any goddamn peasant woman can feed a baby,'' Walter had said. ''But not you!'' And now she was grateful, for they were still high and firm. Her waist was not as slim as it had once been. She turned sideways, looked at her bottom and frowned. There was no doubt, it was a . . . well, you'd hardly call it a *large* bottom, but if you were absolutely honest you couldn't call it a small one, either. ''What the hell,'' she said out loud, thinking ''I'm thirty-four years old. I'm five foot eight. I'm a big, grown-up girl. If I had thin thighs and a tiny bottom, I'd look ridiculous.'' Then this defiant mood left her and she wondered who would care anyway.

The mirror seemed to envelop her. There was something *naked* about hotel bathrooms, she thought. They had always turned Walter on. He was forever wanting to share the shower or bath with her, or to come in while she was dressing. He would pretend to be shaving or brushing his teeth, but she would see him watching her in the mirror.

At first she had been flattered and she had wanted him as much as he had wanted her, for her physical appetite was large. But Walter's idea of love-making had its ethos in the comic-strips. He liked to make love under water or against a door or in the back seat of a car. He would have liked to be the first man ever to do it free-falling. That was his style and she had come to hate it.

And now thinking about Walter brought back the fear. She stopped brushing her hair and listened. Susie's voice was murmuring in the bedroom and she gave a small sigh of relief.

She put on a pair of jeans and a loose-fitting white sweater and finished making up her face. Like her body, it was a map of her life and some of it was good and some bad. Her hair was a dark, rich red, almost black. No grey in it yet. Her face, more attractive than pretty. Hazel eyes and a good skin. An English skin. Not peaches-and-cream or roses, but a smooth, olive-tinted skin which was not being turned into leather by too much sun. There was something to be said for living in a lousy climate. But there were crows' feet at the corners of her eyes and wrinkles were beginning to show on her neck and there would be lots of scarves and roll-neck sweaters in the future. Her mouth was wide . . .

Susie interrupted the catalogue. "Miss Blackstock wants sausages. Sausages and chips and peas, please."

Jane looked at the menu. "They don't have sausages. What about a hamburger?"

"Miss Blackstock doesn't want a hamburger."

"Or fish. You like fish."

"Miss Blackstock doesn't want fish. She wants sausages, chips and peas."

"We'd have to go downstairs."

"You promised. You said Miss Blackstock could have sausages today."

Jane hazily recalled some such promise. But going downstairs would mean taking the elevator and crossing the lobby to the coffee-shop. What could happen in a brief journey like that? She could wait by the elevator until other passengers came, and ride down with them. The lobby would be full of

8

people, but if she held tightly to Susie . . . Walter would never dare to try anything in such a crowded place.

"You promised," Susie repeated.

"All right," Jane finally capitulated. "But I'm going to telephone Grannie first."

She sat on the bed and took off her left ear-ring and dialled the thirteen numbers that would connect her instantly with her mother, three thousand miles away. She heard the telephone ringing. She knew exactly where it stood. It was an odd feeling, being in New York and yet seeing so clearly the interior of the Hampshire cottage. Her mother had bought it when her husband died. After Jane's marriage, she and Susie had stayed there several time, though only once with Walter. She remembered the Christmas when her brothers, Derek, who was in the Navy, and Ben, who was an architect in London, had been there, too. It had been the first time Walter had met her whole family.

It was also the first time she had seen him against her own background. He had bought a new three-piece tweed suit at Harrods which had cost him nearly six hundred dollars. Her brothers had worn old anoraks, shabby corduroys and rubber boots. Walter realised he looked like a *New Yorker* advertisement for Scotch whisky, and he had not liked it.

"Jesus," he had said later. "Don't you feel smothered?"

"What do you mean?"

"You people seem to feed off each other."

"We're close, that's all."

"In my family, it was like World War III all the time." He had made it sound like a virtue.

They *were* close, she thought. Not claustrophobically so, as he had suggested; they had their arguments like any other family. But underneath the arguments and the need for their individual freedoms was a bond which held them together. They kept in constant touch by letter or telephone. At the centre of that bond was her mother, gentle, undemanding, but always there when needed. She could see her now, crossing the long, chintzy sitting-room, the fire blazing at one end, to answer the telephone; or perhaps hurrying down the staircase from her beamed, low-ceilinged room. It was twelve o'clock on a November night in England, her mother had made her promise to phone no matter how later it was. As she waited she thought of the house with its small garden and stream. Susie often played in the garden on summer days with Jane and her grandmother keeping an eye on her. Jane longed to be back there. It was a place of happy memories and emotional support.

"Hello?"

"It's me," she said.

"Darling! I've been waiting for your call. Is it finished?"

"Yes, it's finished."

The moment she had introduced Walter she had known her mother had not liked him. Nor had Derek, nor had Ben. No one had criticised him, but she had known. Because she valued loyalty, especially between husband and wife—she despised couples who complained about each other's short-comings to friends and relations—she had felt obliged to defend him, even after the first fight. No, not fight. If one wanted to be accurate, the word was assault. But finally she had to admit to herself that her marriage to Walter had been a disastrous mistake.

"Signed, sealed and delivered," she said.

"Thank God. And Susie?"

"She comes back with me. I've got her here."

"I've prayed for this. Was Walter there?"

"Naturally."

"You sound guarded. Is Susie listening?"

"She's sitting beside me."

"How does she feel about him?"

"She wouldn't talk to him."

Outside the court, after the hearing, he had squatted in front of Susie, had fumbled for her hand, his flushed face close to hers, frightening her. She had pulled away and hidden behind Jane, burying her face in her scarf.

"Was he angry?"

"Naturally. He lost."

"I mean about Susie rejecting him."

Jane remembered his face, corrugated with rage. "Yes. That didn't help."

"I'm sorry. Was there a bad scene?"

"Kind of."

"What happened?"

"I can't talk about it now."

"Are you still coming home the day after tomorrow?"

"Yes. I wish I were leaving this minute, but I couldn't count on it being over so quickly and we have the booking for Thursday."

"Your room is ready. And Susie's. Can I say hello to her?"

"Hello," Susie said, taking the receiver.

"Hello, my darling. Are you all right?"

"Miss Blackstock saw a blue man and a red man. Miss Blackstock is having sausages and chips and peas."

"That's nice. Chips are called french fries over there, I think. I had some fish for my supper. Look after Mummy and bring her back safely."

Jane put the telephone down and found she was trembling. It was over. She could believe her marriage was finally over now that she had told her mother the verdict and Susie was safely beside her. But her sense of unease had not lifted. Somewhere out there was Walter: waiting, planning, just as he had done before.

She would never forget the day she had gone to fetch Susie from her nursery-school in London and found Walter had already taken her.

"He said he was her father!" the young teacher had said, aghast at Jane's reaction.

"You *knew* we were divorced!"

"But . . ."

"Don't you understand what's happened?"

She had scarcely understood it herself. She had stood

staring numbly at the girl, trying to force the fact into her mind: Walter had kidnapped Susie. After a few minutes, a kind of instinct had taken over and forced her into action, though later she had little memory of her movements. She knew she must have run into the head teacher's room and telephoned the police. They came and went quickly—she must have given them the information they required. Then she had called her lawyers, answering much the same questions.

Alone in her flat that evening, she had gone into Susie's room and looked at the toys left scattered on the floor from the night before; at the small dresses hanging in the wardrobe; at the monstrous face which Susie had drawn on her blackboard and Jane herself had labelled 'Mummy.'

Then she had sat on Susie's bed and cried.

With the tears had come her determination that, whatever it took, she was going to get Susie back; that Walter, although he was the child's father, had by this action abrogated his right to her.

The next day came confirmation of what she had already suspected: he had taken Susie to New York and he did not intend to give her up. Jane had flown at once to America.

Weeks of loneliness and uncertainty had followed. Her attorney had warned her not to do anything which might prejudice the court against her, to make no trouble, to rely on the due processes of law.

"We'll get her back, Mrs. Hemming," he had said. "In a case like this, the mother is always in the stronger position. It's a rare judge who would award custody of a four-year-old girl to the father."

These had been long, costly weeks and she had known that when they ended she would almost have reached the end of her financial resources. But her mother and brothers, who had kept up her spirits as well as they could with their frequent telephone calls, had told her not to worry about money: they would provide whatever she needed, for as long as she needed it.

Two weeks before the case was due to be heard, Walter had telephoned her.

She was shocked by the strength of the fear which rose in her at the sound of his voice, and had to fight an urge to slam down the receiver.

But he was uncharacteristically hesitant and conciliatory.

"I'd like to see you," he had said. "Will you meet me?"

"No," she said, flatly.

"Listen, I've been thinking. I realise that I should never have taken Susie the way I did. I—I guess I was distraught at the thought of losing her. But instead of all this bitterness, couldn't we come to some civilised arrangement? I mean, fighting over her is so bad for *her*. Can't we meet and talk about it?"

It's so bad for her. That was the phrase which had influenced her. Some residual guilt about depriving the child of her father, which had been lying dormant since the kidnapping, fought its way to the surface.

"Please!" he said.

What would be the harm in seeing him? She had been told that, despite his action, a judge would probably grant him reasonable access to his daughter. If they could at least decide between themselves on a basis for agreement, the case might be less painful, especially for Susie.

"Meet where?' she had said cautiously.

"I'll come to your hotel."

"No!" It was an instant reflex. She was not going to be alone in a hotel room with Walter.

There was a brief pause, then he said: "Have lunch with me, then. Meet me at one in the Carnegie Bistro."

She knew the Carnegie Bistro. The tables on the glassed-in terrace were sufficiently far apart to allow private conversation, but there were always plenty of people around. She agreed.

Jane spent the next few hours dreading the meeting, but when the time came it was like talking to a stranger. He no longer mattered to her. But Susie did.

It was not until their orders had been taken that he said: "Have you thought about what I said on the phone? That we should come to some arrangement ourselves instead of allowing Susie to be dragged through the courts?"

"What arrangement are you suggesting?"

"I thought first that she could spend six months with you and six with me. Then I realised that was expecting too much. What would you say to having her in England for nine months each year and letting me have her for the three summer months?" He had leant forward to put his hand over hers. "Jane, you can't expect me to give up my daughter altogether!"

His eyes were sincere and she had felt a touch of pity. Even through the courts he would probably be granted reasonable access. She realised she had never heard Walter plead before.

"Well . . . ' She hesitated.

His voice went on: "I've been wrong. I realise it's too late for you and me to get back together, but don't cut me off from Susie."

"I suppose we could come to some private arrangement, but it would have to be through our attorneys," she had said, slowly.

"Of course! Any way you like."

Considering the alternatives, she had stared out through the windows at the lunchtime crowds hurrying by on 7th Avenue. Then something had interrupted her focus. She blinked, realising that she was seeing Walter's reflection in the window glass. There was a cold smile of satisfaction on his lips, and she realised why he had been called Mr. Fixit by his company. He had softened her up, as he was accustomed to softening politicians and town-planners.

It was too much to bear. Deliberately, she set her napkin beside her scarcely-touched plate, and stood up.

"Good-bye, Walter," she said, and walked out.

That was the last time she had seen him until they faced each other across the court-room. Afterwards, she would sometimes wonder whether, in his arrogance, he had actually convinced himself she would not fight for her daughter. But she knew that the judge's verdict was a public defeat he would never forgive. His ruling had been absolute: " . . . to be brought up by her mother in England." It sounded fine, but was it possible?

Early on, she had learned to fear him for herself. Now she was even more afraid for Susie, for it was she whom he wanted. "Do you really believe this is the end?" he had said as he followed her down the court-room steps. "Do you really believe it? I'm her father, goddam it."

When she had first left Walter and fled to London with Susie, he had followed, trailing her so assiduously and remorselessly that she had been forced to apply for a court order preventing him from persecuting her, while she set divorce proceedings in motion. He had obeyed the letter of the order, but had found his own subtle way of harassing her.

Living with Susie in Hampstead, she had soon become aware that a man was following her. He was short, with a ragged thatch of black hair and flattened Asian features; a man difficult to miss, even in a crowd. She had guessed at once that Walter had employed him to check on her movements with Susie. At first she had wondered why he made his presence so obvious, but then she realised that Walter *wanted* her to recognise the man, to know that she could not escape him. He was always there, standing outside her block of flats, following whenever she went out. He made no attempt to speak to her, but he was there, day after day, week after week. She sensed impending disaster and it was then that she began to wonder if the harassment was only a foretaste of something worse to come. At first the suspicion that Walter might attempt to kidnap Susie was so bizarre that she had dismissed it. As time passed, and the watcher continued to haunt her, his eyes, like flat black pebbles, became part of her nightmares. She saw Susie in his arms and he was running away from her. She chased him, but he drew further and further ahead and, slowly, he turned into Walter, shouting triumphantly as he stole her child.

During the day she had been able to rationalise her fears. Walter was, she knew, a man of potential violence; it had burst through his civilised veneer several times during their marriage. But he was also cold, calculating and ambitious. He would not jeopardise his career by an action as rash as kidnapping. Or so she told herself. But at night, lying in the darkness, her conviction was swamped by her fears and she would often hurry into Susie's room to make sure she was safe.

The pressure had its effect on her. She started smoking again. She lost weight. She became nervous and irritable. Finally, she went to the police. They listened sympathetically, but pointed out that the man had not molested her and that she had no proof that her husband had employed him. There was nothing they could do. She had taken Susie to stay with her mother. The man had followed. But here she had allies. Her brothers had taken it in turns to watch the watcher, making sure he knew what they were doing. And then the local constable, an old friend, had "leant", as he called it, on the stranger until finally the pressure was reversed and he had disappeared.

After a few weeks, believing that Walter had accepted defeat, she had returned to London. And then her nightmares had become fact.

With an effort, she brought herself back to the present.

"Ready?" she said.

Susie tucked the yellow scarf under her arm.

"Don't you want to go to the loo?"

"Miss Blackstock's been to the loo."

"Then, let's go."

The long, silent corridors were empty, their flowered carpeting deadening footfalls. They reached the elevators. There were four cars, usually quick to answer a signal, but now they all seemed to be in the basement. Jane could hear a

16

television along the hall and then, suddenly, a rattling noise which brought her heart into her mouth. She held Susie's hand more tightly.

A man came out from a recess at the end of the corridor and she poised to run. But he was carrying an ice-bucket. The rattle had been made by the ice-machine.

When the elevator did come, it was empty. It was that dead time of early evening and the lobby, usually crowded with new arrivals and flight crews checking in, was silent. The bell-captain sat at his desk, picking his teeth, and there was only one clerk behind the reservations counter. He was a big man named Tony, who came originally from Bombay. When she had checked in and given her address in England, he had been unusually friendly. Part of his youth had been spent in York-shire and he still held a British passport. It gave them some-thing in common, he implied. But now, as she crossed the wide, empty spaces of the lobby, he did not look up.

The coffee shop lay at the far end of the reception area. Half of it was closed and in darkness. The rest contained only four customers. Outside, it was trying to snow. They sat at the counter, Susie settling her scarf on the stool next to her.

"Hi!" the waitress said, putting menus in front of them.

"Do you have sausages?" Jane said.

"Only what's on the menu."

She moved off to serve another customer with coffee. There were eight different varieties of hamburger available, but no sausages.

"But I want sausages, please," Susie said, and there was a dangerous note in her voice. "You promised."

Jane talked rapidly. "Why don't we leave the sausages until we get home? They have better sausages where Grannie lives. She'll cook them for us."

"I want sausages *now*!" Miss Blackstock, the Prince, Sir Henry were forgotten. This was a direct confrontation between Susie and her mother, and Susie wanted sausages. In a way, Jane felt the child was testing her, trying to find out whether the mother to whom she had just been returned was,

17

at this early stage, going to let her down. As Walter must so often have let her down.

"Made up your minds?" the waitress said.

"My little girl wants sausages . . . '

She was not unfriendly, but she shook her head: "There's only what's on the menu."

Susie's eyes filled. She's tired, Jane thought. Tired, emotionally overwrought, bored with hotels and being pushed around. What have we done to her?

"Listen," the waitress said, "half a block south there's a coffee shop called O'Hare's. Try there."

That meant going out of the hotel. It was dark now, and sleet battered against the big plate glass windows that faced the side of Carnegie Hall. The early evening crowds were hurrying home, bent against the wind. She looked at her unhappy child. Oh, hell, they should be safe enough. She decided to risk it.

"We'll try O'Hare's," she said. "Thanks."

They emerged onto 7th Avenue. The wind buffeted them, the sleet stung. She turned right and saw the sign. O'Hare's was only seventy or eighty yards away.

"Can I share Miss Blackstock?" she said. She wrapped the scarf twice around Susie's arm and gripped it with her right hand, turning it around her wrist and tying them together. It would be difficult for anyone to wrench the child away from her now.

At O'Hare's, they ordered sausages.

When they came, Susie said: "They're not the same as Grannie's. I don't like them."

"What do you want then?"

"Ice cream."

Jane ordered her a sundae and stared out at the sleet. The window was curtained half way up and she could only see heads as people scurried past. Someone stopped and eyes peered through the glass. The disembodied head was a white blur, then it was gone. Susie said: "That's the blue man."

"Finish your ice-cream." She longed to get back to the hotel room, to put the chain on the door. The room had become her territory and, like an animal, she sought its safety.

"The red man and the blue man," Susie was saying to the scarf, which was folded into a small square on her lap. "Miss Blackstock knows the blue man. He looked at her through the window just now, but Mummy didn't notice. He was on the big steps. With the red man. Miss Blackstock remembers."

The words penetrated Jane's mind. "What steps?" she said sharply.

"The steps today."

"You mean the steps outside the court? Is that what you mean?"

"The long steps."

"What's all this about the red man and the blue man?"

"Miss Blackstock doesn't like the red man."

"Which was he?" It was as though a hand tightened in her stomach.

"He took me away."

"Walter?"

"I don't like Walter."

"Who was the blue man?"

"The blue man came with Walter."

"Why do you call Walter the red man?"

"His face was red."

"And the blue man? Did he have a blue face?"

"No, silly! A blue coat."

Something pricked at the edge of her memory. A blue man. She tried to build up the picture in her mind. She had gone down the court-house steps first, holding Susie, and her lawyer had been with them. And then . . . and then Walter had come down, taking the steps two at a time until he had caught up with them. He had grabbed Susie's hand and crouched down . . .

No, that was too far on in the action. Go further back.

19

Walter had called her by name. They had been ahead of him, half way down the steps. The lawyer had told her that there was a limousine waiting for them. Then Walter had called. She had turned.

Someone had been standing next to him. They had come out of court together. A man in a blue coat? No. Not a coat. A blue parka. Walter had spoken quietly to him and then come down to Susie.

Her body went rigid as she recalled the incident and she felt her hand shaking so much that she had to put the coffee-cup down on the table. Who was the man in the blue parka? He was not Walter's lawyer. She knew *him*. She tried desperately to set a face on top of the coat, but could not.

"What did he look like?" she said.

"Who?"

"The blue man. What did he look like?"

Susie's eyes slid past her face. "That's him," she said.

"Where?"

"At the window."

Jane swung round.

"He's gone now," Susie said.

"Are you sure?"

"Miss Blackstock's sure."

And Jane was sure, too. He was one of Walter's men. They had to get out of O'Hare's. But what if he was waiting for them? What if he knocked her down in the crowd and grabbed the child? She had heard of people being bundled into cars in the middle of New York and no-one attempting to stop the kidnappers. She had read of a shooting in full daylight, while passers-by hurried away, unwilling to become involved. Was that how it would happen? Was that what the man in blue was gambling on? Would he simply come up and force Susie away from her while everyone looked the other way?

The coffee-shop door opened. She looked towards it, terrified she was going to see the man in the blue parka. But it was Tony, the Indian from the hotel. He wanted to order a

20

pastrami on rye to take away. Urgently, she waved for her bill and paid.

She waited for Tony to pick up his sandwich, then she took Susie by the wrist and hurried across the room.

"Hello," she said. "Do you remember me?"

He turned.

"I'm staying at the hotel. I'm from England. We talked, remember?"

He was a big man with a black moustache and he smiled with pride at being addressed by such an attractive woman.

"I remember. You coming from London."

"And you once lived in Yorkshire."

"Correct. Correct."

"Are you going back to the hotel? I promised Susie I'd ask if you'd give her a piggy-back."

"Packabag?"

"Miss Blackstock didn't . . . "

Jane interrupted her smoothly. "A ride on your shoulders."

"Surely!" he was pleased.

She indicated the bag holding his sandwich. "I'll carry that."

He scooped up the child and put her on his shoulders. They walked up 7th Avenue. Jane thought she saw a man move into the hallway of a building and disappear into the shadows, but she couldn't be sure. Susie rode above the heads of the crowd, laughing delightedly.

They crossed 57th Street. Jane looked around. All she could see were hurrying people, and then they were in the bright, warm lobby of the hotel.

At some point during the evening Miss Blackstock gave place to the Prince, and Susie fell asleep telling the scarf an involved story about a Chinese magician who travelled to London on a camel.

Jane pulled a chair up to the window and looked out over the canyons filled with lights. But the windows seemed to

21

stare back at her and she drew the curtains and shut out the city.

She lay on her bed, her mind filled with thoughts and images, fragments of sentences, words, all racing round and round, trying to catch up with each other.

Questions appeared like the neon signs that illuminated the room, winking on and off. Where was Walter? What was he planning to do? Where would he do it? When would he do it?

He had threatened to take Susie away from her again and she had no doubt he would, given the chance. Had the man in the blue parka hoped to kidnap her this evening? Or was he only spying out the land? No one, surely, would try an abduction in an hotel which had a large security staff. She had only to pick up the phone to call for help. And there was no way she would open the door to anyone tonight. But once she left the hotel, she was vulnerable. There were nearly forty-eight hours until their aircraft was due to leave. Would Susie only be safe if they stayed holed up in the room? And then there was the journey to Kennedy. How was she going to get there? By limousine? By mini-bus. Should she take a cab? Whichever route she chose, there would be a risk. This was Walter's town. He knew the alternatives better than she. His plans were probably already made.

She realised that her imagination was overheating, but she was incapable of restraining it. Walter was a violent man. She *knew* how violent he was. Once he struck her so hard she nearly lost her hearing in one ear.

The worst thing was that she also knew he wanted Susie not because he loved her, but because he regarded her as one of his possessions. After he had brought her to New York, he had left her in the care of a housekeeper and she had hardly seen him. Walter's background was small-town Midwest. He had rarely spoken about his parents, but from what he had said she saw them as quarrelsome, semi-literate, living just on the poverty line. He had left home at seventeen and, by a mixture of aggression, determination and ruthlessness, started his climb to success. The possessions he had acquired on his way up symbolised that success: his ostentatiously furnished home; his paintings and antiques; Jane and his child.

She had first met him when she had been working in London's Universal-President Hotel, and he had come from the United States on hotel business. For a long time after they married, she had accepted his own definition of his job: trouble-shooter for Universal-President Hotels, Inc. The chain prided itself that it really was universal, with hotels in every major city in the world, and Jane imagined him as a kind of specialist in labour relations, who had to be ready to fly off at a moment's notice to deal with problems in Paris or Vienna or Hong Kong.

It was only after they had been married for a year that she learned his work had nothing to do with labour. He was, in fact, in charge of the chain's slush fund. When UPH wanted to build on a prime city site which had already been scheduled for a hospital or a school, it was his job to fly out there and make sure the schedule was re-arranged. He contacted people whose signatures were needed. If there was anything shady to be dug up in their pasts, he found it and used it. If not, he entertained them, played a little golf or took them skiing in the Guadarramas or yachting in the Mediterranean. And soon, mysteriously, they acquired a second home in Sardinia or Corfu; or a BMW; or a minor Picasso. UPH rarely had to abandon plans for a new hotel.

He knew how to arrange such matters in foreign countries, so how much simpler it would be for him to organise a kidnapping in his own city. Snatching a four-year-old girl and whisking her out of Jane's reach would be easy compared with bribing the erratic chief planning officer of a simmering development area.

By the time Susie was born, Jane had already had experience of his ungovernable temper and had been on the verge of leaving him. For Susie's sake, she had decided to give their marriage another chance, hoping against hope that the child might mellow him. Then one day when Susie, little more

23

than a year old, had a feverish cold and had been crying miserably for an hour, he had gone to her cot and drawn back his hand to slap her into silence. Jane had jumped in front of him and received the blow. The next day, he had left on a trip to the Middle East. By the time he returned, she and Susie had flown back to England.

She could go to the police, she thought, but what would she tell them? That the child's father had . . . what had he done? No one had heard him threaten her or Susie. And the man in the blue parka? She knew nothing about him, would not recognise him. They would think she was mad. During her brief marriage she had lived in Westchester. She had no friends on New York City. Even her lawyer was purely a professional contact and, in any event, he had already left for a Bar Association meeting on the West Coast. There was no one to help her.

She slept fitfully that night, but by morning had come to a decision. Walter would certainly have checked on her flight booking. She had to get Susie out of New York some other way. Once they were away from the city, she could make alternative arrangements to leave the country.

2

Susie was sleeping on her right side, knees drawn up, a flush on her cheeks, her mouth half open. The scarf was crumpled up and she was using it as a pillow. It seemed almost criminal to wake her, but at eight o'clock Jane called her name softly. She stirred and rolled on to her back. Instinctively, even before she came to full awareness, her hand went out, feeling for the scarf. There was a moment's apprehension on her face and then, as her fingers closed on it, she opened her eyes.

"Time to get up," said Jane.

"Are we going home? Are we going to see Grannie?"

"Not yet. There's been a change. First we're going to a place called Boston."

"Why?"

"Because . . . well, you know what it's like when you stand in a queue in London waiting for a bus and they won't let you on because they're full up. You have to wait for another one. That's what's happened with the aeroplane."

"It's full?"

"That's right. So we're going to take one from Boston instead."

"Have I ever been to Boston?"

"No."

"Have you ever been to Boston?"

"A long time ago."

"Is it nice?"

"Very nice."

Susie jumped out of bed, pulling her scarf with her, and went into the bathroom. Jane began to pack her clothes. Yes, she had liked Boston. She had been fourteen years old and her father, a Royal Navy Commander, had been one of a

25

team that had attended a two-year course at the US Navy's Oceanographic Institute at Woods Hole on Cape Cod. Jane had been at boarding-school in England and had joined her parents in the long vacations. She could not remember much about Woods Hole, except that it overlooked a horse-shoe bay and in the summer months was overrun by tourists waiting for the ferries to Martha's Vineyard and Nantucket Island. One Christmas they had rented an apartment in Boston, and she had loved every minute of it. Her father was on leave and her brothers were there and they had gone to restaurants and movies and theatres and shopped in Filene's Basement, where she had been almost smothered in the Christmas rush. It had been a good time. Nothing had gone wrong. The result was that Boston, for her, had a safe, warm, friendly association. More important: she had never been there with Walter. As far as she could remember, she had not even told him about her stay there. There was no reason for him to suspect she would leave from Boston.

While Susie was in the bathroom she ordered breakfast and then, once more, stood at the window. Her fears of the night before were, temporarily at least, damped down by a new optimism: the windows she could see were no longer eyes, but simply panes of glass, and through some were shirt-sleeved men working at desks, women behind typewriters. It all seemed normal and safe. She felt ashamed of allowing her imagination to run away with her as it had the night before. But earlier, as she had looked down at her sleeping daughter, it was not imagination that had dominated her. She had known, in the most simple and basic terms, that she could never give Susie up to Walter. Even though the forests of the night, with all their terrors, had given way to comforting daylight, he was still a threatening figure, somewhere out there. But now, she felt, she could match her wits with his.

In the early hours of the morning she had remembered how she had once suggested to him that instead of flying from Paris to the Côte d'Azur, he should take the Blue Train. He had looked at her as though she was out of her mind.

"Trains?" he had said. "Who travels on trains?" To him, the only conceivable form of travel was air, first class. So assuming his people—for she guessed there would be more than one—would be covering the flights out of New York, she had decided to take the train to Boston. She hoped it would simply not occur to him to have Penn Station watched.

Amtrak's "Minuteman" was due to leave New York at 11.30 am. She reckoned it was about ten minutes by cab to the station, so at 10.45 she and Susie left the safety of the room and went down to the lobby. She could feel her stomach clenching. Again she twisted the scarf so that it formed a rope binding Susie to her.

As she stepped out of the elevator, she saw a man standing nearby. He was wearing a blue parka. She stopped and tightened her grip on the scarf. He had his back to them, and Susie had not seen him. And then she saw another man in a blue parka entering the door of the hotel. And a third walking along the pavement. Everywhere she looked she seemed to see men in blue parkas. She felt panic rise: one man she could deal with, but four or five . . .

She told herself not to be silly. Dozens of men in New York wore blue parkas in winter—but, that being so, how could she hope to identify her enemy?

A voice behind her said, "Good morning, Madam!"

It was Tony, his teeth gleaming white against his brown skin and black moustache. "Are you leaving us?"

"Yes."

"What a pity. I was thinking that we could be having dinner together, perhaps. With the little girl, of course. Have you been to the Top of the Park?"

Taken aback she said, without thinking: "No. I mean, I'm sorry, but we have to go to Boston."

"It is a beautiful restaurant."

"Perhaps another time."

"Well . . . " He shrugged philosophically and made as if to pass her. She said suddenly: "Is there another way out of the hotel?"

"Sure." He pointed to the far end of the lobby. "Go there and take a left . . . "

"I meant, without going through the lobby. There's someone I don't want to see. A man."

"A man?"

"He's been pestering me."

"Pestering?" Tony looked aggressive. "I'll give him pestering! Which one is he?"

She pointed in the direction of a man standing near the revolving door. He was wearing high boots, a Texan hat and a string tie. He was well over six feet tall and built like an oak door.

Tony swallowed. "You want me to . . . ?"

"All I want is to avoid him."

"You follow me." He opened a door next to the line of telephones. "Staff quarters," he explained.

She followed him down a long passage that led past the kitchens. Soon they emerged through an exit onto 56th Street not far from 8th Avenue.

"Are you wanting a cab?"

She nodded and he flagged one down. "Don't forget," he said, passing in her two suitcases, "next time you and Tony will be having dinner."

"Where to, lady?" the driver said.

"Penn Station."

"New Haven! New Haven! The train is now entering New Haven. Thank you for travelling Amtrak. Have a pleasant day and better tomorrows."

Jane woke with a start as the train slowed and stopped. She felt a rush of panic. For a second she did not know where she was, and then she looked to her left and saw Susie curled up, asleep, in the big red plush seat. Her relief was balanced by a feeling of guilt. She must stay awake. And when they reached Boston she must remember to call her mother and tell her they would not be arriving at Heathrow as scheduled.

The train went on into the cold, grey afternoon and after a

while Susie woke and Jane read her "The Cat in the Hat". The dense scrub forests gave way to more open country, some of it marshland, and she began to have glimpses of the sea. They passed New London, then Mystic, with the tall masts of the wintering yachts etched against the sky like a steel engraving.

Susie was looking out of the window and Jane watched her with troubled eyes. It was only when you had kids that you began to appreciate your own parents. She hoped she would react as well as her mother if Susie suffered the same problems as she had.

She had been a child of the sixties and had grown up with Flower Power, the Beatles, the Stones and marijuana. It had been smart to smoke pot at her boarding-school and the fact that she did not like it, that it made her feel ill, had not helped when she and six other girls had been caught. NAVAL OFFICER'S DAUGHTER IN DRUGS ORGY, the local paper had screamed, and she had been expelled.

Her parents had been wonderful—or, at least, that's how she saw it now. Then, she had been in the middle of the teenage rebellion and had resented their civilised attitude. At seventeen, she had decided to push them to the limit and told them she was going to Katmandu. Instead of trying to stop her, they had given her money and urged her to take care. She had travelled through Turkey and Afghanistan with a group of kids all following the hippie trail, but she had never really been one of them; she was too fastidious to enjoy a life where one was expected to live in a kind of floating commune, where the food was poor, sex was shared and where there was never enough water to have a bath. By Kabul she had been ready to quit, but had not known how to go about it. Hepatitis had saved her, if that was the word, and she was flown back to England, where she spent nearly a year recuperating. Again she had expected recrimination from her parents, again it had not come. Everyone just seemed pleased to see her back in one piece.

She had taken a long time to recover. Later that year her

father died and she had need of her renewed strength when, for the first time, her mother had allowed herself to take, rather than give support. They had moved to the cottage in Hampshire. Her brothers had already left home and her mother had taken a job in the nearby market town of Petersfield, to fill her time. Jane, without skills, was left to mind the house and wonder what she wanted to do with the rest of her life. She got up late because she could think of no better way to pass the day; she read; she watched a television movie if there was one; she did the shopping; she took the dog for walks. Occasionally she went to the local disco, but the boys there seemed very young and gauche after the experiences of her own life.

She became bored and restless, though she did her best to hide it, guilt-stricken at the thought of her mother's loneliness if she were to leave.

Then, soon after her twenty-first birthday, her mother had said, casually: "How would you feel if I were to go away for a while?"

"Away?"

"I had a letter from Jean yesterday." Jean was her older sister, who lived in Canada. "She feels I need a change and she's asked me to go on a cruise with her."

"How do you feel about it?" Jane asked cautiously.

Her mother shrugged. "I don't like the thought of leaving you alone in the cottage."

Trying not to show her sudden interest, Jane had said: "I think you should go. It would do you good. I'd go to London for a while. Maybe do a secretarial course, then find a job."

Within a week they had arranged to let the cottage for a year and Jane had found a flat in West Hampstead and enrolled for an intensive course at a secretarial college. Much later she discovered that her mother had organised her affairs to achieve precisely this result.

She had loved being in London and by the time her mother returned it was tacitly accepted that they would continue to live apart, though Jane went to Hampshire most weekends. She had worked hard and spent nearly nine months learning office management, shorthand and typing, how to master word-processors. She began to dress differently. Ankle-length printed cotton dresses gave way to skirts, cashmere jerseys and high heels. She had her long hair shortened and began, for the first time, to use make-up. Soon she looked exactly what she was: a decorative, efficient private secretary.

She had worked for some years for an advertising agency in Mayfair, rising steadily in the hierarchy. Then she had shifted to a senior job in the public relations department of Universal-President Hotels.

She was able to buy a car and move from her studio-flat in Pimlico into a three-room apartment in Chelsea. Social and professional success increased her self-confidence and polished her natural charm. She acquired a wide circle of friends and had played as hard as she worked, indulging from time to time in a series of brief, undemanding but pleasant love-affairs.

Then she had met Max Ingram, a painter of birds and animals, and had fallen in love with him. He had widened her social horizons to include the art-worlds of Chelsea and Hampstead and, chameleon-like, she had adapted to his way of life. Her wardrobe had become less conservative and, almost unconsciously, she had begun to add touches which gave drama and gloss to her appearance.

Soon Max had virtually moved in with her, though he retained his studio in Fulham. They had become an established couple, invited everywhere together. Though they did not discuss the future, Jane had taken it for granted that some time—say, if they were to decide to have a child—they would marry.

Later, in hindsight, she could recognise the danger signals that presaged the end of the affair. At the time, she had been too blind or too complacent even to suspect the reason behind his longer absences in his studio, his sudden cancellation of arrangements, his non-appearance at parties where he had agreed to meet her, the increasingly long periods between love-making.

Then he had told her he had been commissioned to illustrate a book about the birds of Africa. He would be leaving almost immediately for Lake Naivasha in Kenya, to paint flamingoes, would travel there to South Africa and be away for several months.

She had waited for him to ask her to accompany him. Instead, he described arrangements which made it clear that he was going alone. She had been too proud to query them.

The night before he was due to leave he had told her, with some tenderness, that he could not bear airport farewells, so they would say good-bye in the flat. She protested that she had already arranged to take the day off, but he was adamant.

In the morning, when he had gone, she had mooched around for an hour, missing him dreadfully. Then, on the spur of the moment, she decided to drive to Heathrow for a final glimpse of him—and to hell with his inhibitions.

Final glimpse it was. She had arrived at the terminal in time to see him making for the departure lounge, his tall, lanky figure immediately recognisable in the crowd. She had hurried towards him, then stopped abruptly. His flight bag was slung over one shoulder. His other arm was around the shoulders of a pretty, fair-haired girl Jane had never seen before. She had watched them pass through the barriers together.

He had written to her once from Kenya, telling her what she already knew. She had not replied and, though she knew from mutual friends when he arrived back in England, he had never contacted her.

She was still smarting from the pain and humiliation of that affair when Walter Hemming had arrived in London.

He was physically attractive, projected an air of sophistication, was a lavish spender (though only, as she discovered later, when he wanted to buy something: in this case, her), and his flattering attentions did much to heal her hurt pride and battered ego. When he returned to the United States he had written to her every week and, a few months later, had asked her to fly to New York and marry him. It had seemed, at the time, to be a good idea.

Their first months together had been happy enough, because he had been away much of the time and each return was a renewal of erotic excitement. At first he would bring her gifts—a cashmere shawl from India, a Hermes handbag from Paris, a lace mantilla from Madrid, champagne, chocolates—and was flatteringly urgent in his love-making. Later, as she looked back on that period, their life together seemed to have been spent mainly in bed. She could remember no conversations, no quiet moments when they were contented merely to be together, no shared amusement. Outside the bedroom, they always seemed to be with other people, for when he was not abroad he found it politic to entertain lavishly. Once again the image she presented to the world changed. To conform with his wishes, she dressed to attract attention and became a reflection of the latest in fashion, speech and attitudes. She always seemed to be busy, playing hostess, flattering Walter's contacts, assuming an almost frenetic vivacity which was altogether foreign to her nature. And yet, although she was constantly meeting people, they were all like passing ships, sailing in and out of her life with such speed that in the end they coalesced in her memory into one blurred, smiling face. She made no real friends and, though she welcomed the opportunity to relax and be her real self when Walter was away, she was lonely and spent most of her time reading, knitting, or writing to her family.

Once he was sure of her, he had begun to change—or, perhaps, to revert to normal. He had no longer bothered to control his vicious temper; his sexual demands had become increasingly esoteric; he had cut her housekeeping allowance while demanding the same high standards of food and drink; he had neglected her for days on end and rumours reached her of his interest in other women. After the first year, it had been downhill all the way.

3

South Station, Boston, in the December dusk. Jane had no memory of it. Except for a yellow Budget-Rent-A-Car sign, it was grey, dingy and very cold.

She had a reservation at the Mayfair Hotel in the Prudential Centre, and they took a cab. The driver, a small black man with greying hair, turned to talk to her over his shoulder. "You English?" She nodded. "From the Mother country!" he said, smiling.

Surprised, she said: "Are you from England?"

"Kingston, Jamaica. But I been here fourteen years, man and boy."

"You still think of England as the Mother country?"

"Sure. Ain't that what it is?"

"Do you like Boston?" she said, feeling obliged to continue the conversation.

"Boston's fine, if you got the cash."

He began a long, rambling story about how he had tried to buy an apartment in the centre of the city but had found the mortgage repayments so high it had been impossible.

She stopped listening and settled back in the seat, holding Susie's hand. The man's voice was curiously comforting, his domestic affairs a world away from her own problems. But the comfort was short-lived.

" . . . sixty-nine cab-drivers," he said.

"I beg your pardon?"

"Sixty-nine. Twenty-nine dead, forty cut up. That makes sixty-nine."

"In Boston?"

"That's right, lady. Boston's got a crime rate just the same

34

as New York.'' There was a hint of pride in his tone.

"Killed? Twenty-nine drivers?"

"Murdered. And some of them that got cut up wishes they were dead. You got my word on that. Junkies. Knife. Gun. Couple guys got hit with hammers . . . "

She felt chilled and looked out with new eyes at the heavy traffic and the lighted buildings. Was this the Boston she had enjoyed so much? Where, as a teenager she had walked the streets day and night without fear? As yet she had still to see a single familiar landmark. Scollay Square was gone and there seemed to be new buildings everywhere. She wondered if they had torn down Beacon Hill yet.

Their room was on the twentieth floor and overlooked the Charles River. The bridges were necklaces of lights crossing the dark water. There were no eyes to watch her here, and yet . . .

She wished, suddenly, that she had a date with someone in the bar downstairs. She wanted to hear the low hum of conversation and laughter, the clink of ice in glasses. She wanted to be sitting in a restaurant, elegant, dimly lit, with someone amusing. She wanted a steak and a bottle of wine and good conversation about anything at all except divorce, custody, maintenance, violence. She needed to be part of a different world, even for a short time, but she knew all along it would be a betrayal of Susie. But no companion was available, and soon Susie, lying on her bed looking at a book, would say she was hungry and demand something which was not on any available menu.

Then she remembered that in her flight bag was a bottle of Canadian Club she had bought to take home to her brother Ben. She could get him another bottle tomorrow at the airport's duty-free shop. So, since this was probably her last evening in America, she would have a drink, or maybe two, and then she would take Susie down to The Old New Orleans Creole Restaurant on the ground floor of the hotel in spite of the fact that it might not have sausages, chips and peas on the menu.

Her thoughts were interrupted by the telephone. She took a hesitant step towards the instrument, reluctant to pick it up. Nobody knew her here. She realised she was on the verge of allowing a ringing telephone to send her into the same kind of panic she had felt in New York. It was another indication of how the strain of the past months had distorted her outlook.

"Hello?"

"Mrs. Hemming?" A man's voice.

"Yes."

"This is reception, ma'am. We've had a malfunction in our computer. It means we have to run your credit-card details through again, I'm afraid. I have to ask you to bring it down. But it won't take a moment."

"Can't it wait? I'll be going to dinner soon. I could bring it then."

The voice was apologetic. "I'm sorry, ma'am. We really do need it now."

She knew nothing about computers except, from her limited UPH experience, that when one did run amok, the consequences in a big hotel chain could be catastrophic.

She sighed. "I'll be down in a minute."

She glanced at Susie, who was absorbed in her book. Her instinct was to take the child with her but, mindful of the dangers of allowing her imagination to overheat, she told herself not to be silly. Over-protectiveness could ultimately be as damaging as Walter's neglect. She would take the key with her; no one could get into the room; she would be back within five minutes.

"I have to go downstairs, darling," she said. "Why don't you have a wash while I'm away, and then we'll go and have dinner in the restaurant."

"All right." Susie slipped off the bed.

Jane went into the bathroom and ran some water into the hand-basin. "There you are. Have a good wash and I'll be back by the time you're finished."

One of the elevators was waiting and she was in the lobby

less than two minutes later. She made for the reception desk.

"I've brought my credit card," she told a girl clerk.

"Credit card?"

"My name's Hemming. Room 2027. Someone from here rang a few minutes ago and asked for my credit card."

"When did you check in?"

"About an hour ago. Is your computer working now?"

"Working?"

Slowly and clearly, Jane said: "The man who rang told me you'd had trouble with the computer and wanted to run my credit-card number through it again. Here is the card."

The girl looked at the card, looked at Jane, then beckoned to a male colleague. "Joe, this is Mrs. Hemming. Did you call her?"

"No."

"You hear anything about the computer malfunctioning?"

"Nope. Everything's fine. Must have been a mistake, ma'am."

"A mistake?" Panic began to gather.

She turned and ran for the elevators.

She reached the twentieth floor and raced through the corridors. When she reached the room, she thought at first she must have the wrong one. The door was open. She looked at the number, 2027, and checked her key. This was her room. She pushed the door. There on the bed was Susie's book. But where was Susie?

She went into the bathroom. The water was still in the hand-basin, clean and sparkling; the soap was dry; the towels unused.

"Susie!"

She flung open empty closets, peered behind chairs, even under the bed. It had to be a game, Susie was hiding. From the door, she looked along the silent, empty passages. A maid, pushing a trolley of cleaning implements, came round a corner.

"Have you seen a little girl—about so high?" Jane called. "Wearing a red sweater and jeans?"

37

Indifferently, the woman shook her head and plodded on.

As the first surge of panic steadied, Jane began thinking constructively. Susie was somewhere on this floor. She *must* be. She hurried along the passage. When she saw doors ajar, leading into unoccupied rooms, she went in, calling Susie's name. She opened doors marked "Staff," and "Private" and "Emergency Exit," and called down concrete stairways and peered into dark cupboards and linen-closets. There was no sign of the child.

She seemed to cover miles of flowered carpeting, passing closed rooms whose fish-eye peep-holes stared blindly at her. There may have been people behind the doors, but she saw no one, heard nothing. The hotel was like a ghost city from which plague had driven all the living inhabitants.

After minutes which seemed like hours, she discovered that she was re-crossing paths, seeing signs she had already passed. By the time she reached 2027 again, she was running.

Her hand was shaking as she picked up the telephone.

Shortly there came a knock on the door. Two men stood outside, each wearing an identification badge.

"Hotel security, ma'am. We understand your daughter . . . "

"I left her here and took the key . . . she was going to have a shower . . . the call . . . a hoax . . . "

"Let's take it from the beginning, Mrs. Hemming." He was youngish, fair-haired, with a square, hard face and a briskly competent manner. The name on his badge was Henry Cassell. "You had a phone call . . . ?"

As succinctly as she could, she told them what had happened, answered their questions, heard Cassell issuing instructions into a walkie-talkie.

"Don't worry, we'll find her," he said. "I expect she wanted to explore. Kids do, you know. You'd be surprised the places they get to. We'll have the whole building covered in a few minutes."

She had not told them about Walter. Why not? Why hadn't she said: "My husband's kidnapped her!" Then she

38

realised she had not told them because she would not allow herself to believe that Walter had taken Susie, that he would be capable of tracing them to Boston so soon.

The two men had disappeared and she sat alone. The room was over-heated, but she was shivering. She seemed to see Susie's small, lonely figure running down one of the endless hotel corridors, growing smaller and smaller.

Afterwards she wondered if she had fallen into some kind of limbo where time stopped, because she remembered nothing of the passing minutes until she heard movement outside. She jerked into full consciousness as a group of people appeared in the doorway: the two security officers, another man she had never seen, and Susie, wide-eyed and smiling, clutching a bar of chocolate.

Jane went down on her knees and put her arms around her, careless of her protest as melting chocolate dripped on to the floor.

It was several seconds before she could control her voice. "Where—where have you been?" she said.

"In the shop."

"What shop? Susie, what happened? Why did you leave this room?"

Cassell interrupted, indicating the third man: "This is Bob Goodliffe, our drug-store manager, Mrs. Hemming. He found her there. She was by herself, perfectly happy, eating her Hershey bar. I told you there was nothing to worry about."

"But she had no money. How could she buy . . . ?"

"The man bought it for me," Susie said.

Jane froze as Cassell said sharply: "What man, honey? There was no man with you in the drug-store."

"He went away."

"Who was he? Where did you meet him?"

"He knocked on the door."

"This door?"

"Before I had my shower. I thought it was Mummy. I opened it and the man said Mummy wanted me downstairs and he'd take me, so we went in the lift and he bought me chocolate.''

"What did he look like?" Cassell said.

"Just a man. He had a funny mus . . . mous . . . " She sketched a moustache on her upper lip with a forefinger, and giggled.

"A small one or a big one?"

"Big."

Cassell turned to Goodliffe, who shook his head. "I didn't notice any guy with a moustache, but the store was crowded."

"Can you remember anything else about him, Susie?"

But she had thrust a corner of the scarf into her mouth and did not answer.

Cassell said: "Are you sure he came to this door, Susie? Sure you didn't go downstairs by yourself and meet him in the shop?"

"He came here. I opened the door."

"And after he bought you the chocolate, he just went away?"

"Yes."

"Did he—touch you?"

Jane held her breath, then expelled it in a sigh of relief as Susie said: "He held my hand."

"Can't you tell us more about how he looked?"

She had finished her chocolate and she'd had enough of questions. She simply shook her head, then climbed up onto the bed and picked up her book.

After a few more minutes, the security men gave up.

As they left, Cassell said: "We're going to try and trace him, Mrs. Hemming, but I don't rate our chances very high. Every hotel gets guys like this from time to time. He must have seen you check in, then made the hoax call to get you out of the room. Fortunately, you acted quickly and he must have been frightened off when the search started. All I can say is, he doesn't seem to have done her any harm."

No, Jane thought, but what if he hadn't been frightened

off? What if I'd been a few moments later calling in? One thing was sure: it had not been Walter, nor the man in the blue parka. There was, she supposed, a kind of comfort in knowing that.

But Boston had gone sour. She'd had enough of big cities, with their lurking threats and latent violence.

She looked at Susie, peacefully studying her comic, cheek resting on her scarf. Suppose the man had . . . ? What if . . . ?

She poured herself a whisky, drank it quickly and gave herself another. Her thoughts went back to the telephone call. The voice? An ordinary American voice with no regional inflection she could identify. And the man Susie had tried to describe? An ordinary man whose only remarkable feature, apparently, had been a moustache. He would be virtually untraceable.

She realised that her desire to see people and be in a public place had gone. She wanted to stay in the safety of her lair. She wanted the door locked and barred and bolted and Susie beside her. She ordered a meal from room-service and was in bed, trying to get to sleep, by nine o'clock.

Boston had changed dramatically by the following morning. The sun was shining. There was a brilliant, clear sky and the Charles River was like glass as an early sculler sent his shell skimming across its surface. At any other time Jane would have been entranced by such a view in such weather, but the events of the evening before lay in the penumbra of her consciousness, leaving depression and unease.

She and Susie had coffee and croissants in the room and then went into the lobby to ask where they could find a travel agent.

The bell-captain directed her to one on Boylston Street. It was a cold, crisp morning and everyone seemed to be wearing parkas, a constant reminder of the man in New York. There were beige parkas and blue parkas and orange parkas and blue parkas . . . and men with moustaches. What had happened to her, she wondered, that she should now see

41

a threat in the most trivial object? Walter, that's what happened. Walter, and a man who had fancied a little girl . . .

She found the travel agency a block away from the hotel. There were two clerks, both busy. While she waited she picked up a travel folder extolling the charms of Cape Cod, began leafing through it.

"Look, English soldiers!" Susie pointed to a splash of red in the window, a poster showing the Changing of the Guard outside Buckingham Palace, and Jane felt her heart turn over with longing to be home.

After a few moments a girl came towards her. "May I help you?"

"I want to fly to London. Two seats."

"When for?"

"Today, if possible."

"There's no direct flight from Logan today, but you could take the shuttle to New York and fly out from Kennedy."

"Is there a flight from here tomorrow?"

"Sure, but there are a lot of people travelling right now." She used the telephone, then said: "You're out of luck. The first direct flight with seats is the seventeenth."

"But that's nearly a week away!"

"Like I said, there's no problem from Kennedy."

"I don't want to fly from New York."

"There's stand-by. But I guess with a little girl you wouldn't want to take the risk of not getting on."

"No."

She waited, then said: "They're holding. You want the seats on the seventeenth?"

Jane made up her mind. "Yes. I'll take them."

Maybe it would even be for the best. Walter would guess that her aim would be to get Susie out of America as soon as possible. He would be unlikely to continue a search for her for more than a day or two when he discovered she had left the hotel in New York. He would assume she was already in England.

At the same time, after last night, she did not want to

42

spend any more time in Boston. Susie, too, would be happier in a less claustrophobic atmosphere.

As the girl finished writing out her tickets, Jane said: "I used to know a place called Woods Hole. Is there a decent hotel somewhere near there?"

"The Cape's pretty much closed up. A lot of hotels and motels stay open until Thanksgiving and then shut down for the winter. But I know Bill Dugan's place in Margate stays open. It's called the Fisherman's Arms and I can recommend it."

Jane vaguely recalled Margate, an attractive fishing-village far out on Cape Cod. A haunt of painters and writers. Why not? As a refuge, both from city life and Walter, it would be ideal.

"You want me to call and see if they have a room?" the girl said.

But she was out of luck again. The line was busy.

"You don't really need to book," she said. "This time of year there's no problem."

Susie said: "The blue man and the red man!"

Jane swung round. When she followed the child's pointing finger, they were two strangers, one wearing a blue parka, the other a red one, but she felt a renewed urge to leave Boston as quickly as possible. She picked up a few more brochures about Cape Cod and they returned to the hotel. From a car rental agency in the lobby she hired a small Ford for a week, then she checked out and made for the south-east expressway.

Once she was clear of the industrial sprawl she drove off the Interstate on to Route 3A, which became like an English road, winding in and out of New England towns and villages, with their white clapboard houses and green lawns. The autumn was over and the trees were bare. She could see the ribs of the landscape and she thought she had seldom seen anything so beautiful. One village followed another, each with its white-painted wooden church. Slowly, she relaxed. Her neck, which for the past weeks had been tensed like a bar of iron, began to soften.

Then she noticed a car, travelling at her own speed, keeping a steady forty yards behind her. She kept an eye on it for five minutes, slackening her speed to encourage the driver to pass, but the car remained in position. It was a dark green Buick and she could see a man's head behind the wheel.

The roads at this time of year were almost empty of traffic outside the towns. She had always hated playing Pied Piper to another car and became increasingly irritated. She pulled over to the side and slowed, waving the Buick past, but it, too, pulled over and slowed down. After a moment, she increased her speed. When she glanced in her mirror, the other car was there again, behind her. What was he trying to do? A race? Pick her up? She saw a narrow road turning right and signalled a turn. As she swung into it, the Buick's right-hand indicator began to flicker. She put her foot hard on the accelerator and sped along, past the neat houses with their stretches of unfenced green lawn. The Buick's speed increased, too, and, as she glanced into the rear-view mirror, she had an impression that its driver was laughing at her.

A T-junction loomed ahead and she swung left, then left again, bucketing back towards the main road. She would be safer there than in an empty suburban street.

Back on Route 3A, Jane maintained her speed, and the Buick stayed with her. The tension that had drained out of her was tightening her muscles again. All she wanted was peace, and she had to pick up a cowboy!

A car approached from the opposite direction and, as it drew nearer, the driver flickered his headlights three times. Was he warning her of a speed trap. She glanced at her speedometer. It was showing seventy, way over the limit. She braked and, as the needle dropped back to sixty—fifty—forty, realised that her pursuer had at last decided to overtake.

He drew level and raised a hand in mocking salute. She looked at him, and gasped. Involuntarily, her hand tightened on the wheel and the car swerved. She was looking into a pair of huge, red-rimmed eyes and a mouth with thick red lips, set into a flat, dead-white face.

They stared at each other for some seconds, then he drew away as she crept along at a steady thirty-five, passing a police cruiser which was parked on the right-hand verge without even noticing it.

It was not until the Buick had disappeared into the distance that she realised she had seen nothing more sinister than a ski-mask, knitted in white wool, the eye-holes and mouth outlined in red. She glanced around at Susie, who was half asleep on the back seat. Fortunately, she had not seen the nightmare face.

It had been a disquieting experience—the second in the space of twenty-four hours—but at least it could have had no relation to what had happened in the hotel.

Until they reached Plymouth just before lunch, she kept a look-out for the green Buick, but there was no sign of it. Almost certainly he had been some local man on his way home from Boston, who had been amusing himself by tormenting a woman driver. She told herself to forget the incident. She and Susie had escaped Walter, they were together. That was the important thing.

The day was even more brilliant on the coast. Plymouth Harbour was flat calm. She pulled into a parking-bay overlooking the water and now, in the gentle Pilgrims' town, surrounded by sightseers, her spirits lifted.

"Look!" She pointed to a sailing-ship which was moored to its own jetty. *Mayflower II* was painted on its side. "A ship exactly like that brought the first English people to America more than three hundred years ago."

"From London?" Susie said.

"Not from London, but from another Plymouth in England. That's why they called this place by the same name. Would you like to go and see the ship?"

"I'm hungry."

"Okay. We'll go after lunch."

They decided to eat at *The Half Shell* on the port and

found a table at a window where they could watch a fishing-boat unload its catch of cod and haddock into a refrigerated truck. The sun slanted through the glass and Jane felt its warmth on her shoulders.

"There are sausages," she said.

"I don't want sausages. I want fish fingers."

"They have real fish here."

They compromised on broiled scrod and Jane ordered half a bottle of Chablis. As she sat sipping her drink, she let the wine and the sun work their magic. It was as though a knot in her brain was beginning to unravel.

By two o'clock there were half a dozen orange school buses parked beside the *Mayflower*, and she hesitated, wondering how long the tour would take. Then she thought, what's the hurry? For the first time in weeks, she had a sense of being her own mistress. She could come and go as she pleased. There were no arrangements to keep: time could be moulded to her own needs. And, best of all, no-one knew where she was. She had cabled her mother that her plans had changed, but gave no more details. There was no way she could be traced.

"Come on, let's go and see the ship," she urged Susie impetuously.

The numbers had thinned when they walked towards the gangplank. A woman in seventeenth century costume, with a shawl and a mob cap, stood waiting to receive them. "Good day to ye," she said. She was in her sixties and wore a pair of wire-rimmed spectacles on the end of her nose. She bent down to Susie. "And whom be you, m'dear?"

Susie looked startled. "Why does she talk like that?" she whispered.

The woman said, "I be Mistress Pengally, from Bideford in Devonshire."

Susie stared at her uncomprehendingly, then giggled.

"This lady is a—a sort of actress," Jane explained. "She's pretending to be a woman who sailed in this ship and settled here more than three hundred years ago."

"Why?"

"Because . . . well . . . "

Suddenly the Pilgrim reverted to a nice, twentieth century matron. Looking around to make sure no-one else observed her temporary abandonment of her role she said confidentially: "It's often difficult for kids to understand."

Jane smiled. "Are you supposed to stay in character all the time?"

"They're very strict about it. We can't even answer questions about anything that happened after the sixteen-twenties, because our characters wouldn't have known."

"Don't you ever make mistakes?"

"Sometimes. And don't think we're not picked up! I was up at the Plantation last year and I was baking bread in one of the 1627 Settlers' houses. A tourist came in and asked me if I was using yeast. I said, 'What be yeast, Mistress? I never heard on it.' I'd thought it was a modern ingredient. Turned out she was a food scientist and she spent twenty minutes telling me the history of yeast and how it had been used from the time of the early Egyptians."

"What's the Plantation?" Jane asked.

"You should go there. It's a reconstruction of the first village in Massachusetts, built in 1627. You can walk around and talk to the Pilgrims and ask them questions. Children love it." She pointed across the road to a perky little red bus standing by the side-walk. "That's the Plantation bus."

"Can we ride in it?" Susie said excitedly.

"Is everyone in costume there, too?" Jane asked.

"Oh, sure."

"I suppose you're all actors?"

"Not at all. Some of us are just interested in the history of Massachusetts and others are descendants of the *Mayflower* Pilgrims."

She glanced around, saw another group of visitors on the jetty and slipped back into her role, smiling down at Susie.

"You didn't tell me how'm you're called, my lass," she said.

Reassured that she was a normal human being, despite her curious manner of speech, Susie told her.

"Susan. 'Tis a fine name. Well, now, Susan, you'm speaking like someone from the Old Country. England."

"Mummy and I come from there," Susie said with more confidence.

"Give me thy hand, then, Miss Susan, and come along with me and I will show thee the ship. Would 'ee like that?"

As they entered the 'tween decks of the *Mayflower*, and looked at the bedding, the eating utensils, the primitive furniture, the open fire on which meals had been prepared at sea and other replicas of seventeenth century artefacts, Jane could see the gradual awakening of her daughter's imagination. Soon, her face turned up to the woman and her eyes shining, she had left the twentieth century behind and was totally absorbed in living history.

As they drove on towards the Cape, Jane heard her graphically describing the ship and its voyage to Miss Blackstock, and she had already extracted a promise of a future expedition to the Plantation, including a ride in the little red bus.

They crossed the Sagamore Bridge over the Cape Cod Canal and it was as though they had left mainland America and moved into a more tranquil world which had little connection with the frenetic, sophisticated, often violent life of the cities.

She took a route along the Inner Cape past Sandwich, Barnstable and Brewster. The sun dipped towards the horizon and the day lost its colour. The country seemed to become more familiar and she realised she must be remembering it from years ago. Even the cranberry bogs at the roadside, with their vines making a close-grown russet mat, seemed to be imprinted on her memory.

There were few other cars on the road and most of the motels were closed. The farther she drove, the more deserted the Cape became. The vegetation changed from hardwoods, which six weeks earlier would have been a blaze of colour, to scrub oak and dwarf pine. She began to see sand dunes with bent sea grass, and colonies of summer shacks boarded up against vandals and the severe Cape winter. After she passed Orleans she began to pick up the signs for Margate, at the very tip of America.

Dusk was falling as they arrived and Jane felt a sense of coming home. She had recognised the name when the girl in the travel-agency had mentioned it and wondered whether she had been here before with her mother and father.

Then she realised that at least part of its familiarity was its resemblance to a small fishing town in England. It was built on two levels, on the sea-shore itself and then on the slopes and the top of a low hill, its houses all higgledy-piggledy and at different levels, its streets winding, some no wider than lanes. Even in the poor light she could see that the wooden houses were painted pink or white or pale yellow. Had they been in brick or stone she might have been looking at a Cornish village.

She found a parking area on top of the hill. It was cold now and night was coming in quickly over the calm, dark sea. She left the car and stood looking out over the scene, the smoke rising from the houses, the sea beyond, dunes away to her right and left and the ozone strong in her nostrils. It was so peaceful it brought a lump to her throat.

As they walked along the main street, Jane realised that it was almost a ghost town. "Sorry, we're closed" signs were everywhere; on shops, restaurants, even bars. Occasionally a neon light stood out in the dusk, but they were few. She went into a pharmacy to ask the way to the hotel. There was only one customer, a well-dressed woman wearing a fur-trimmed grey suede coat and matching boots, who was having a prescription filled, tapping her fingers impatiently on the counter as she waited. Her cool, dark eyes studied Jane and Susie for a moment, then she looked away. She did not return Jane's polite greeting, though the pharmacist, a plump, genial man in a white jacket, called that he would not keep her waiting long.

49

"I'm afraid I'm not a customer," she said apologetically. "I was wondering if you could direct me to the Fisherman's Arms."

"Sure. Take a right at the end of the street, towards the beach. The hotel's to your left, past the jetty."

"Right, then left. Thank you." She turned to go.

"The hotel is closed," the woman said. She had a strong foreign accent.

"Closed? Surely not. I was told in Boston that it stayed open all year."

"Only the restaurant is open." She turned back to the counter. "Is this going to take long?"

"It'll just be a moment, ma'am."

"Is that true?" Jane asked him. "Is the hotel closed?"

"I have told you so," the woman said.

Jane was suffering from a case of instant antipathy. She disliked the woman's sleek appearance, her expensive clothes which belonged more to Boston than to a fishing village, her arrogance and calm assumption of knowledge about which there was no argument. She reminded Jane of the women who had been part of Walter's world.

She went towards the door, hearing a protesting squeak from Susie as she was pulled along more quickly than she liked. "I believe we'll go and see for ourselves," she said.

The woman half turned, shrugged, and made a dismissive gesture with her hand.

4

It was already dark when they arrived at the Fisherman's Arms—a wooden building facing the harbour beach, weathered to a dark silver in the winter gales and hot summer sun. It was three storeys high, with a rambling, sandy look, slightly rusty and wind-blown. Jane found it charming but she involuntarily reflected how much Walter would hate its simplicity. The thought was another thread of security. She no longer had to worry about Walter's feelings.

There was a light over the door and the windows were made of green bottle glass. She went in and found herself in a wood-panelled lobby which was warm and friendly. There was a group of paintings on the walls, Cape Cod views, almost abstract in their economy of line, the reds and hot pinks of summer and autumn, the ice-blues and browns of winter.

There was no one about, but she saw a door marked "Restaurant", and went through into the dimly-lit room. Obviously, it was too early for any diners to have arrived, but the tables were already laid. It was a big, marvellous room, like a stage-set awaiting the actors, built out over the sandy beach, within fifty yards of the fishing-harbour with windows on three sides and a great round Spanish fire-place in the middle on which two massive logs were burning. On her right was a small bar. A man was rearranging bottles on one of the shelves behind it. He heard her and turned.

"Hi," he said.

She stood staring at him, dumbfounded. For a moment, she thought she was looking at Max Ingram. He was probably in his mid-thirties, and had the same tall, spare

51

frame, the same angular face; but where Max's hair had been wispy, this man had thick, dark hair, greying at the temples. There was an amused expression round his mouth.

"Dinner?" His hand closed on a menu and he looked down at Susie. "For two? Would you care for a cocktail first?"

"I'd like dinner a little later. What I want now is a room."

"I'm sorry, but the hotel's closed for the season. We keep the restaurant open, but not the rooms." His voice was deep, with a touch of the Boston twang she had always associated with the late President Kennedy.

"Damn!" She could not hide her disappointment, which was mixed with irritation at finding the woman in the pharmacy had been right.

Some of the lights went up in the restaurant and a chunky, bearded man wearing a white cotton tunic and light grey striped cotton trousers came through a pair of swing doors. He stopped when he saw her.

"We don't get enough custom to keep on a full staff in winter," the tall man explained.

"Someone in a Boston travel agency said you were open all the year."

"They were wrong, I'm afraid."

"We've always stayed open before," the bearded man said. He came towards them, but she sensed that the remark had been directed more to the bar-tender than to her. "We've always made out. This is the first winter we've closed."

She was becoming annoyed. "Don't you think you should let the travel agents know, so that people don't come all this way for nothing?"

"Which travel agents?" the tall man said.

"I went to a place on Boylston Street this morning. The clerk specially recommended the Fisherman's Arms. She seemed to know you. You are Mr. Dugan, aren't you?"

"My name's David Maclean. I bought the place from Bill Dugan a couple of months ago. This is Peter Davidson." He gestured towards the bearded man, and smiled. "He's the real boss. He cooks and he's teaching me the business."

52

If it was meant as a conciliatory gesture to the chef, it failed. His face remained expressionless.

"Is there anywhere else I can stay?"

"Not in Margate." He turned to Dickinson. "What about Truro?"

"There's nothing much before Chatham."

It was dark now and she had been driving for most of the day. She had found what she had thought was the pot of gold at the end of a rainbow: a friendly little fishing-town of the sort she had not thought could still exist in America. And the hotel: warm, comfortable, idiosyncratic. She was tired. Susie was tired. She wanted a drink and a meal.

Maclean must have sensed her unhappiness, for he said: "I'm sorry. I'd like to help."

"She could have the beach cottage," Dickinson said.

Maclean shook his head. "It's not ready for guests."

"I don't care what it's like," she said. "I just want somewhere to stay."

Sensing a conflict she didn't fully understand, Susie began to snuffle, looking up at the men with wide eyes which Jane knew from experience were likely at any moment to become tear-washed. She had thrust a corner of the scarf into her mouth.

Dickinson said: "How ready is ready? There's linen. Only needs the heating turned on."

"I don't think . . ."

There was a tension between the two men on which Jane had no hesitation in capitalising. She did not flatter herself that Dickinson was taking her side because he felt sorry for her. He was interfering in Maclean's decision-making for reasons of his own.

"I wouldn't want any service or cleaning," she said. "We'd do it ourselves, wouldn't we, Susie? It won't be for long." Then, recalling hotel owners in the past who had resented guests who ate away from their own dining-rooms, she added: "And we'd have our meals here."

Maclean began to speak and she felt sure that he was about

53

to refuse her, but then Dickinson said to him: "You want to come into the hotel business, you got to learn the first rule: flexibility. The customer's always right, sport."

Maclean's face tightened, then he nodded. "Okay, you guys, have it your way."

She directed her smile of gratitude towards Dickinson. "For this relief, many thanks!"

He returned her smile and went back into the kitchen. There was something about his attitude that told her he had won a small victory.

Maclean escorted her to the cottage, making no attempt at small-talk. It was a few hundred yards away from the hotel, along the beach. A short, concrete path covered in blown sand led up to the back door from the street. It comprised a sitting-room, a bedroom, a bathroom and a kitchen which led off the main room and could be hidden by dropping a bamboo blind. Most of the furniture was built in and there were two large divans covered in cushions in the sitting-room. It had been designed for summer use and was cold and damp, with a slight smell of sea-weed, but it was comfortable and functional. Maclean told her Dugan had built it as a guest-house for his friends.

He switched on the heating and soon warm air was blowing through the rooms. As Jane turned on lights, he found bed-linen.

Susie watched them, the corner of her scarf still in her mouth.

"It won't be long now," Jane told her. "We'll have supper and then I'll tuck you up in bed in your very own room. I'll sleep in here. But first we'll go and fetch the car."

"Where did you leave it?" Maclean said.

"In the parking lot on the hill."

"I'll get it."

"There's no need for you to go. Susie and I . . . "

"She's beat," he said. "Give me the keys."

She passed them to him. "That's kind of you. It's a white Ford Escort."

"I turned on the hot water. You should have it in twenty minutes."

At the door he paused. She thought he was going to speak, but after a moment he turned away.

"Look, I'm sorry if this is an inconvenience," she said. "I didn't mean to start anything at the hotel. It's just that it was exactly what we had hoped to find, and I was disappointed. We've been . . . well, we've been on the move rather a lot lately. I hope it's not too much trouble having us here."

He smiled. "No problem. I'm new to this kind of life, that's all. Peter's right: flexibility is the watchword. How long will you be staying."

"Until the sixteenth, I think. We leave Boston for England the next day."

Half an hour later she and Susie were back in the restaurant. A group of three men at the bar were the only other customers.

Maclean took her to a table in the big, sea-facing window. "Feeling better?" he said.

"Much. There was enough hot water for a shower."

She was wolfishly hungry and her steak was good. Susie, too tired to be demanding, ate an omelette without protest. When she had finished, Jane sat over the last of her wine and watched the three men at the bar. She amused herself by trying to guess their backgrounds and occupations. Two were dressed in expensive, self-consciously arty clothes. One wore dark blue linen trousers, with a toning silk shirt and a carefully-knotted red scarf at the throat. The second wore strawberry-coloured denims and a loose, matching shirt with a Mao collar. The third could have come from a different world. He had a two or three days' growth of beard, wore rubber boots, dirty yellow oilskin trousers and a heavy white fisherman-knit sweater over a plaid work shirt. Yet they were obviously friends and, from what she could hear, were talking about fishing. Occasionally one of them would glance over in her direction, but they made no attempt to approach her.

"Enjoy your meal?" Maclean said as she stood up to leave.

"Very much. Mr. Dickinson does a good steak."

"I'll tell him. No coffee?"

"There's only one thing I want now, and that's bed."

A wind came up during the night and she could hear surf breaking on the beach. Susie was asleep in the bedroom and she herself was warm and comfortable on one of the divans. She listened to the wind and the sea and she felt safe and protected.

She woke to a room full of orange sunlight. The travelling clock on her bedside table showed 7.50 am. Turning on her left side she could look through the bedroom door and see the mound under the blankets where Susie lay. She would let her sleep on for a while, largely because she did not want to get up yet herself, nor even to move; her body was like soft butter. She had slept for more than eleven hours.

This was what she needed; what they both needed. A few days of this and they would be as good as new. She began to plan the day. She could do anything or nothing, just as she pleased. Even her fear of Walter was fading.

The sun eventually forced her up. On such a sparkling day it seemed almost immoral to lie in bed. She had a feeling of excitement she had not experienced for a long time; a desire to explore new territory.

On the way to the bathroom she saw that a note had been pushed under the front door. She looked at it suspiciously. It worried her to think that someone had come to the cottage and she had not known. Why would a note be left in an apparently empty dwelling? Then she saw that it was addressed to her and she breathed more easily.

She picked up the envelope, opened it and read: "Dear Mrs. Hemming, I forgot to tell you that the restaurant does not open until evening and I didn't want you to be without your breakfast coffee. Look outside the back door. Cordially, D. Maclean."

She unlocked the stiff, warped door with some effort. There was a cardboard box on the step and she carried it into the kitchen. It contained coffee, rolls, butter, two sorts of jam, a box of cornflakes, milk, a carton of eggs and a packet of bacon. At the bottom was a card which read: "Compliments of the Management and to make up for a rather grouchy start."

On impulse, she picked up the telephone, and dialled the hotel.

After a moment Maclean's voice said: "Fisherman's Arms."

"Good morning, D. Maclean."

"Good morning, ma'am." She heard him chuckle.

"I've never seen such an amount of food. I haven't had bacon and eggs for breakfast in a long while, but I'm going to cook some now. It was very kind of you."

"You're welcome. Here on the Cape we eats well and we drinks well."

"I can see that."

"There are a couple of snack joints in town that might do you for lunch. We'll look forward to seeing you this evening."

"Thank you again."

"Have a good day."

She woke Susie and had a shower and cooked an enormous breakfast of bacon, eggs and hot rolls. When they had finished Jane asked her what she would like to do.

"Miss Blackstock wants to see the boats," replied Susie.

"That's what I'd like to do, too."

The wind had slackened but there was still a fresh breeze blowing off the sea, so they wrapped up warmly and went out of the cottage's front door. Jane paused and looked about her, sniffing the air like an emerging animal. There was a wide sun-deck from which they could step straight on to the beach. The view was the kind she liked best, an intimate, busy landscape—or, in this case, seascape. The beach was not very big. There were forty yards of sand between cottage and sea and it was about a quarter of a mile long, bounded by a promontory at either end. It was a working rather than a pleasure beach. Nets were drying on it, dinghies were being refurbished and repainted; there were piles of floats and coils of ropes.

The hotel was on her right, facing the small port, which consisted of a sea wall and a jetty, with moorings on either side for a total of ten or twelve fishing boats. Only four were there now and one was unloading its catch, which was being packed into a refrigerated truck parked on the jetty. A cluster of squawking, fighting seagulls rode the waves around the boats and there was a strong smell of sea, fish and Stockholm tar.

She took great gulps of the cold, briny air, enjoying its cleanliness after the fumes of New York and Boston. Susie raced ahead of her along the beach, dancing and whirling, her scarf a flag in the wind.

"Look at me! Look at me!"

She ran on until she reached the jetty. "Be careful!" Jane called, ploughing through the heavy sand.

Susie ran out on to the jetty and disappeared behind the truck. Jane hated to have her out of her sight and hurried after her. She was climbing the steps on to the jetty when she heard a voice shouting: "Hey! Hey, you! Scat! Get lost!"

Susie shot out from the far side of the truck. She was clearly terrified. Jane lifted her and held her tightly.

"That man!" she gasped.

A figure stepped from behind the truck. "You want to watch that kid, lady."

"What do you mean by frightening her like this!"

"I mean, you want to watch that kid. You let her run off by herself and one day she's going to get hurt."

"She wasn't doing you any harm!"

He was one of the men she had seen in the hotel the night before: the one dressed in the dirty oilskins and rubber boots; the one who had not shaved for some days. His face

58

was still covered in stubble. He was of medium height and heavily built and the most noticeable things about him were his hands: big and strong and scarred.

"We got machinery here could break kids to pieces."

"You can see she's only a little girl. You've frightened her."

"Okay, well . . . I'm sorry. But better be safe than sorry."

She put Susie down and they left the jetty. "Let's go and explore the town and see if they have any ice-cream," she said.

The incident might have blighted the morning, but the day was too good, the town too beautiful and their spirits too high. They window-shopped, they ate ice-cream and they walked along the top of a line of cliffs to the north of the town. In the distance she could see a long beach and a light-house.

After a hamburger at a snack bar she said: "Shall we go back to the cottage for a while?"

"All right."

She had to wrestle the door open again. She thought she must remember to mention its stiffness to David Maclean because if it warped any further it might not open at all. Susie climbed onto her bed with her scarf and a comic book and soon fell asleep.

Jane had run out of reading matter, but there were some old copies of the *New Yorker*, and she flipped through them. When she had finished she placed them on a low, square coffee table in a neat pile. She looked about her. It was restful, relaxing, but time was going to hang heavy if they had to spend too much of it indoors.

She decided that the best thing for her to do was plan each day, morning and afternoon, building up to dinner at night. That would be the high spot. Seafood or steak, half a bottle of wine, and then . . . well, then she would not mind so much spending the evening alone, reading. So . . . this afternoon they would walk on the long beach she had seen . . . back to the cottage . . . Susie could watch TV . . . a drink, then

59

dinner. Tomorrow they would explore some of the other Cape Cod towns by car.

By mid-afternoon it had begun to cloud up and the sea had turned choppy in a blustery northwester. There was only one other car by the long beach where she parked, and the owner was nowhere to be seen. It was a grey sand shoreline and in the distance was the white finger of the lighthouse which, she had discovered from a map, was called Shoal Point. A ridge of dunes ran parallel to the beach and the wind was bending the grass that grew sparsely on the crests. A concrete path about four feet wide wound in and out of the dunes. "Look, there's a natural trail," she said. "Would you like to walk on that?"

"I want to go on the beach."

The sand was heavy, so they walked down near the water's edge where it was firmer. Susie ran on ahead, picking up seashells. Jane thought of calling her back, then realised there was no need. Not another soul was visible; no stranger to be carefully inspected. Again she felt the unfamiliar sense of security.

Not that she did not have problems to face. Now that one problem had been solved it was as though the very solution was uncovering others. She strolled along, absorbed in her thoughts. For the past months she had been so wrapped up in the present that the future had been left to look after itself. But now it had arrived. There were plans to be made, decisions to be taken. Where was she going to live, for instance? Initially, she would return to her mother's home, but that could not last long; she would have to find a place of her own. And then there was money. What if Walter did not pay the alimony she had been awarded—which seemed highly likely? She would have to sue him for it. Was she prepared for yet more litigation? She had some savings and a little money from her father's estate, but it was not enough to keep herself and her daughter for very long.

Susie dashed up to her, holding a shell. "What's this?"

"It looks like a periwinkle."

"And this?"

"Clam, I think."

"Miss Blackstock found them."

"Good for her."

The child ran off again.

Money . . . she had some jewellery Walter had given her. She could sell that. What else? A job, of course. But how to work and still give Susie the security she needed. Most important of all, she must make sure that the court order which she had been granted to ensure Susie's safety was still valid. Only the possibility of proceedings against him, and the subsequent threat to his career, might be enough to dissuade Walter from carrying his vendetta to England.

Apprehension crept over her as she took stock of another aspect of her future. Could she live alone for ever? The thought dismayed her. She had been happy with Max, though they had hardly ever done anything together which could remotely be construed as exciting. To be with him, to love him and believe she was loved by him had been sufficient. She had been contented enough even with Walter in the early days, and simply enjoyed being married. But now she found herself torn between her instinctive aversion to a future on her own and reluctance when she contemplated the stresses inherent in any new relationship. There had been too much emotional stress already. Then she thought, oh, hell, I'll just take life as it comes for a while.

"What's this one?" Susie said.

"Looks like a mussel."

"And this?"

"I don't know, darling. American shells are different from ours."

"I think it's another periwinkle."

"Okay, it's a periwinkle."

How Max would have loved this place, she thought. She had seen more than a dozen different species of birds in less than half an hour. But Max was not here. Idly, her thoughts moved on to the man who had brought him back into her mind. David Maclean. The physical resemblance was superficial and she now realised that the momentary *frisson* it had caused had nothing to do with nostalgia. It had been, rather, dismay at the reminder of her first serious emotional mistake. First Max, then Walter. Two disasters. There would not be a third, she told herself grimly.

"Look!" Susie was pointing towards a dune.

A man was standing there, watching them.

Jane glanced over her shoulder, but the beach stretched away emptily behind her. He began to walk towards them, his feet sinking into the soft, dry sand, a dark figure against the white background, with the light behind him.

"Give me your hand," Jane said. As she turned to retreat, he waved. A greeting, or a peremptory order to stop?"

"It's the other man," Susie said.

"Which other man?"

"From the hotel. Who pours the wine."

Maclean. She took a deep breath and let Susie's hand drop. He was dressed in a dark blue corduroy windcheater, a tweed cap and heavy twill trousers. A pair of powerful Zeiss binoculars hung round his neck. He came towards them in slow motion through the heavy sand and there were some seconds of embarrassment as they watched each other but were still too far to greet without shouting.

As he reached them he said, "Hello, Mrs. Hemming. Hi, Susie."

"We were going for a walk," said Jane, unnecessarily.

"It's just as well to do it now. It's going to get colder—but there's a saying here: if you don't like the weather, wait a minute."

She smiled and indicated his binoculars. "Bird-watching?"

He nodded. His face was thin and hawklike under the cap, but his eyes were friendly and the smile lingered around his mouth.

"It's a bird-watcher's paradise," she said. "I knew someone who painted birds. We used to watch them for hours."

"I'm just a beginner."

"I've seen a dozen species in the past half hour. But there are one or two I didn't recognise. Maybe you could identify them . . ."

"That's a nice collection of shells," he said to Susie, cutting across Jane's inquiry.

"This is a periwinkle."

"So it is." He turned back to Jane. "You want the lonely sea and the sky, or could you stand company?"

"Company would be welcome."

"I was hoping you'd say that."

They walked on in silence for a while, then he remarked: "There's something about this place that gets to you. Have you noticed yet? Maybe it's the remoteness. I don't mean in summer, it's pure, overcrowded hell then, but now. It has a kind of bleak beauty you don't find anywhere else."

"You don't find it too lonely?"

"It's not all that lonely. There's always—something going on." She had the feeling that he was watching her more closely than was natural, almost as though he was assessing her reactions. When she did not speak he said, more briskly: "We're not really cut off from the rest of the civilised world. Did you know that the beginning of Route Six is right out here?"

":Route Six?"

"You can travel on it to Cleveland and Chicago and Denver, through Utah and Nevada clear across the continental United States to California."

"You sound like a Kerouac character."

"You've read his books?" He sounded surprised and looked at her with new interest.

"Only *On the Road*."

"That's *the* one. This is where he really should have started his journey. It's a romantic book, but it tells you more about America and the Americans than any other book I know."

"Talking of books, I've run out of reading matter," she said. "Is there a bookshop open in town?"

"Sure to be. If there isn't, I have dozens. I stocked up for a long winter."

They went on, talking little. The only sounds they could hear were the hiss of the surf and the damp sand spattering under their rubber soles. When they had covered a mile or so Susie began to flag and they turned and walked slowly back the way they had come.

"What made you buy the Fisherman's Arms?" Jane asked idly.

He shrugged. "It was for sale. I like the area."

"Somehow you look as though you'd be more at home in the city."

Again she thought she saw his look sharpen, but after a hesitation so slight she decided she had imagined it, he said easily, "How should I look?"

"Oh—more like that man in the bar last night."

"Which man?"

"The one in sea-boots and oilskins."

"And unshaven?"

"No. It's just that he seemed to fit better into the landscape."

"I could always have an anchor tattooed on my forearm. Would that help?"

She laughed. "Or *Mother*, with hearts and flowers. No, I'm afraid a tattoo wouldn't be enough." She studied the sensitive face, the penetrating dark eyes, the frame that gave an impression of wiry strength. "All I can say is, you don't look or sound like a typical English landlord."

"How would you describe *him*?"

"Oh, hearty, red-faced, gregarious, hail-fellow-well-met."

"No," he said thoughtfully. "I wouldn't have said that described me exactly."

"You're difficult to place."

"Mysterious?" he said hopefully.

"Sort of."

"Maybe it's because I'm a kind of hybrid. I've lived abroad a good deal."

"Where?"

"Paris. London. Among other places."

"Doing what?"

"It's your guessing game."

"I'd say you were . . . you don't look like a business man, either. Something professional? Architect, perhaps?"

"You're getting closer."

"I give up. What *did* you do?"

"Law."

"An international lawyer? How exciting."

"Not quite."

"What, then?"

But he had stopped walking and put the binoculars up to his eyes. At first she thought he was looking at a cormorant diving offshore, but she followed the angle of the glasses and saw that he had focussed on a fishing-boat coming around the point, dipping and rolling on the short, choppy sea, making for the harbour.

"You'll have to excuse me. I must go," he said abruptly. Before she could reply he had walked swiftly away. Within a minute she saw him get into the other parked car and drive off.

"Well, that was rather sudden, wasn't it?" she said.

"Why did he go?" asked Susie.

"I don't know. Perhaps he wants to buy some fish."

The same three men were at the bar when she took Susie to the hotel for dinner that evening. Maclean was pouring their drinks.

They stopped talking as she entered and watched her move down the room towards the tables. She nodded as she drew level. They were not an attractive trio: two of them over-dressed and the third, who had frightened Susie, still in oil-skins and sea-boots, with a heavy sweater, though he had shaved.

To her surprise, he smiled widely at them, and stepped forward. "Hey, look, here's my princess!" he said. Susie tried to draw back, but before Jane could stop him he had

65

picked her up and sat her on the bar top. "This is a real princess!"

Susie put a corner of her scarf into her mouth and stared at him with big eyes.

"I heard a noise at the truck this morning," he went on. "You know who it is? The princess here. She gave me a fright. I gave her a fright. No hard feelings, princess. Let me buy you a drink . . . " He was not entirely sober. His eyes were bright and his manner exaggeratedly expansive. "What's it going to be? Seven-Up? Dr. Pepper?"

Susie shook her head.

"Come on, now. We're all friends here. You're English. Dennis is English." He pointed to one of his friends, the middle-aged, bald man who wore tight strawberry denims.

Maclean broke in. "Let me introduce you, Mrs. Hemming. Frank da Souza. Your fellow-countryman, Dennis Pate. Willi Fischer."

Pate's body was soft, round, almost feminine, and his pale tan had come from a sun-lamp. There were traces of powder on his cheeks.

"How do you do, my dear? It's not often we have the pleasure of an English visitor at this time of year." His voice was light, his manner avuncular.

Fischer spoke with a marked German accent. He was thin, with sunken cheeks, a thick head of wire-like grey hair and eyes that were embedded deeply in his skull. "Please," he said, bowing over her hand. "You will allow us to buy you a drink."

Realising it would be both rude and embarrassing to refuse, Jane asked for a gin and tonic. Susie settled on a Seven-Up. For a while the conversation was general, about how crowded the Cape was in summer, how difficult it was for the residents to settle down to work.

Maclean, who had moved to the far end of the bar and opened an account-book, did not take part, but once or twice when Jane glanced at him, she had the impression that he was missing nothing.

Pate and Fischer, it transpired, had lived in Margate less than a year. Fischer was a painter and Pate was writing a biography of Aubrey Beardsley which would, he said, cover the scandalous and hitherto unsuspected aspects of the artist's life. They talked glossily about a Rothko retrospective in Boston, about the new design movement in Los Angeles, Hockney's swimming-pools, Isherwood's guru, Lichtenstein's change of direction. They tossed the conversation like a tennis ball between them, producing points of view, dropping names, telling anecdotes in such a way as to suggest they had themselves been part of the action.

But Jane, remembering the art-world she had entered during her affair with Max, began to detect false notes.

She found herself comparing the painters and writers she had known, in their shabby corduroys and sagging shirts, with these two, who looked as though they had ordered wardrobes from Sulka or Brooks Brothers to fit an image they wanted to create. She thought how embarrassed Max would have been by them. Da Souza was clearly out of his depth and had lapsed into a sullen silence. He drank steadily.

Pate was talking about his book again. "You see, dear, we don't really know a great deal about Aubrey's inner life. That's why this new material is so valuable. Was he a transvestite, or not? We must go to his drawings for enlightenment. That's the way I'm approaching it, from the psychiatrist's point of view." He paused, then suddenly changed the subject: "Tell me, where are you from?"

"London, mostly."

"Whereabouts in London?"

"Hampstead."

"Which part?"

"I lived in West Hampstead first, then the Village."

He smiled, and she caught a glint of gold in his mouth. "Won't you have another drink?"

She shook her head. "No thanks. We must eat. Susie should be in bed soon."

Peter Davidson, in his white tunic, was standing at the

67

door to the kitchen, watching the group at the bar. As she passed, she surprised a look of contempt on his normally expressionless face.

He followed her to the table in the window. "Seafood Diablo's the special tonight," he said.

"That sounds good. What is it?"

"Oysters, clams, lobster, pieces of fish, done in a piquant sauce on a bed of noodles."

"I'll have it, please. And I'd like some wine. Susie will have sausages."

He lingered. "How are you finding the cottage, Mrs. Hemming?"

"It's fine."

"I hope I wasn't out of line suggesting it. It's not really meant for hotel guests. Maybe you'd be more comfortable in Hyannis."

She looked at him, surprised. "Really, I like it."

"This place dies out of season. You might find it pretty boring after a day or so."

She began to wonder whether he was regretting his insistence that she should have the cottage because it had exacerbated problems between himself and Maclean.

"I spent holidays on the Cape when I was a child. I love it in winter."

"Is your husband in the States, too?"

"I'm divorced."

"I'd have thought a lady by herself would prefer Boston."

He was friendly enough, but Jane was tired of fending off strangers' curiosity.

"Well, I don't," she said shortly.

She had a distinct impression that people kept trying to put her off this town. First that foreign woman in the pharmacy, then Maclean, who had not wanted her to stay; now Davidson seemed to think she was foolish to stay.

He went towards the kitchen, signalling for the wine list on the way.

Maclean suggested she should have a Californian *Chenin*

68

Blanc with the spicy seafood, and then he said, "I'm sorry I left you flat this afternoon."

"It's all right."

"No, it's not all right. It's just that—I suddenly remembered something I had to do."

"You don't need to explain."

He nodded, and as he went back to the bar she felt a touch of regret. He had seemed an intelligent amusing man, but his abrupt behaviour had created a restraint between them, blighting what might have been a pleasant friendship.

The men at the bar finished their drinks and left. She and Susie were the only customers. As they ate their meal Maclean stayed behind the bar, polishing glasses. Peter Davidson put his head around the kitchen door once or twice, but did not come back to the table. They were so clearly waiting to close that she shook her head when Maclean asked her if she wanted coffee.

"Is it always as quiet as this in winter?" she asked.

"I wouldn't know. It's my first winter here." Then, almost nervously, he said, "Look—we'll be closing soon. Will you let me buy you a brandy or a liqueur to make up for my boorishness this afternoon?"

She saw fatigue on Susie's face. But it was only just after eight o'clock. She had at least two hours to fill in before she could even contemplate bed herself. It was probably foolish to make an issue of his momentary rudeness. Anyway, he had apologised.

"Why don't you come and have a drink with me," she said. "I haven't had any visitors to the cottage. I can't give you a liqueur, but I have some Canadian Club—and coffee."

He relaxed and smiled. "I'd love to. Let me close up and I'll be over in half an hour.

Susie was asleep before he knocked on the door. It was the first time she had entertained a man in her own place for longer than she could remember. As they had walked on the beach, laughing together, comfortable with each other, she had felt an attraction to David such as she had not

69

experienced since the early days with Max. Analysing it, she had decided that he was a man for whom she would never need to play a part, as she had with Walter and his circle and even, to a lesser extent, with Max. He had seemed so natural and straightforward that his subsequently curious behaviour had been the more surprising. She told herself as she tidied the room and lit the two table-lamps that she must not over-react.

The lamps' subdued glow gave the room an elegance it did not have during the day, like candlelight on a woman's face. Glasses and ice were on the sideboard, ready for the whisky, and there was a smell of fresh coffee from the kitchen.

"Come in," she called. "It's not locked."

She heard him wrestle with the door. When he had pushed it open, he said, "I didn't realise how badly warped it is."

"I was going to mention it to you."

"I'll have it fixed, but you shouldn't leave it unlocked. Sorry I'm late, but some guy wanted a room. Wouldn't take no for an answer."

"Like me?"

He laughed and put some books he was carrying down on the table. "Peace offering."

They included paperback thrillers and a couple of hardbacks. He picked up one and handed it to her. "To remind you of home."

"Saki! I haven't read him for years."

"One of the best short stories is 'The Unrest Cure.' Should suit you."

"What do you mean?"

"I have the impression you're here because you're in need of a rest cure. I hope it won't be an unrestful one."

Was there a hint of something oblique in his tone. Or was she imagining it?

"I remember the story," she said.

"Are you?"

"Am I what?"

"Having a rest cure?"

70

"Do you drink Canadian Club?"

"I drink most things."

She gestured to him to help himself while she went into the kitchen. She found herself wondering about his questions. Everyone seemed to have questions; everyone seemed to speak with hidden meanings. Why should David be so insistent on knowing her reason for coming to Margate? She poured coffee and took it into the sitting-room.

"Tell me about those three men," she said, turning the conversation away from herself.

He looked at her in silence for a moment. "What do you want to know?"

"Is Mr. Fischer really a painter and is Mr. Pate really a writer?"

"As far as I know. Why?"

"They seem unlikely. I used to know a few painters. They didn't dress like that or talk like that. And da Souza doesn't fit in at all."

"Frank owns a fishing-boat. The other two have latched on to him for local colour, I guess. A genuine native."

"With a name like da Souza?"

"There's a flourishing Portuguese colony around here. A number of Portuguese fishermen settled on the Cape in the last century." Then he said, "You haven't answered my question."

"What question?"

"Let me put it another way. Here we are at the tip of Cape Cod in winter, with everything closed, and out of nowhere comes a beautiful Englishwoman with a small daughter and a nervous tic . . . '

"I haven't . . . " she began, but he ignored her.

"She won't let the child out of her sight, she constantly looks over her shoulder, as though someone is following her."

"Let me freshen your glass."

"She's a mystery," he said. "I love mysteries, but only when I can solve them. If I were one of the local writers, I'd make up a story about her. Title: 'Woman on the Run'. How about that?''

He was speaking lightly, but the edge had sharpened.

He went on relentlessly: ''Now we have to figure, on the run from what? Police? Doesn't seem likely with a little girl in tow. From a love affair? How does that sound? Warm or cold?''

''This afternoon you said I was in the guessing business. Now it seems that you are.''

''I gave you clues.''

''No clues from me.''

''So I go on guessing. On the run from a love-affair? I think not. You didn't react convincingly.'' He looked at her directly and she felt the shock of his eyes. ''Marriage?''

Suddenly she was annoyed. ''What gives you the right to question me like this?'' she demanded.

He looked startled. ''Whoa! It's only a game.''

''Not any longer.''

The gradually increasing sound of a marine diesel broke into an uncomfortable silence. He stood up and moved to the window.

After a moment she joined him, already ashamed of her irritation, not knowing how to apologise.

''Do they fish at night?'' she said.

''It's the best time.''

They watched a boat, with its riding lights swaying from the mast, slowly nose into the jetty and tie up. David turned away.

''You must be tired. I won't keep you up,'' he said. ''Will I see you tomorrow?''

She nodded. ''We'll probably go to the beach again in the afternoon and come over for dinner.''

He left by the door that faced the sea. She watched him move in the direction of the hotel and disappear into the shadows. The lights on the fishing-boat gave a Christmassy look to the harbour and she felt a tug of nostalgia. She wanted to be in England for Christmas.

She picked up the glasses and the coffee-cups, rinsed them and put them away. Tidied up. Checked Susie. She looked at her watch. Nine-thirty. She switched on the television, but the few channels available all seemed to be showing old movies she had already seen. Again she was caught by a feeling of apprehension. Was this what it was going to be like for years on end? Putting Susie to bed and then switching on the TV? Watching it by herself? Was she ever going to have a chance to get out, meet intelligent, normal adults, without fear of what could happen to her child when she wasn't there? It was early, yet David had made an excuse and left almost as abruptly as he had this afternoon. Had *she* driven him off?

Her eyes fell on the books on the table. She would read 'The Unrest Cure' again. She needed cheering up. But why had he used the title as an excuse to probe into her life? And what was *he* doing here? He had admitted to legal training, had lived in London and Paris. Yet here he was, attractive, intelligent, sophisticated, running a small hotel in a backwater. She amended that: *playing* at running a hotel. Her own experience told her that his approach was that of an amateur. Yet he did not seem to have any other interests relevant to life on Cape Cod in winter, did not appear to paint or write or sculpt or even fish. He had claimed to watch birds as a beginner, but had instantly dismissed the subject from their conversation.

When she looked out of the window again, the fishing-boat was dark, but there was a light at the back of the truck which was still parked on the jetty. She thought she could see signs of life. As she watched, another movement caught her eye. A man emerged from the shadows near the hotel and crossed the beach in the direction of the tideline. It was a reasonably bright night with a half moon that appeared every now and then from behind scudding clouds. The figure was tall and wide-shouldered, slightly stooped, and she knew she had watched the same man walk away from her only a short while before.

He went to the edge of the water, then turned towards the

73

jetty. But instead of climbing the steps, he disappeared from view into the shadows of the supporting piles.

"You must be tired," he had said to her a few moments before. She had thought it showed concern, but she had been wrong. He'd had his own plans. A woman? A married woman? Perhaps that would explain the abrupt departure. Someone he could only meet at odd times in safe places. The more she thought about it, the more she felt sure it must be so.

5

A new weather system arrived in the night, bringing in colder air, and when she woke she could hear eddies of sand being blown against the cottage walls. She pulled up the blinds and saw that there were very few people moving about the harbour.

"What about some shopping today?" she said. "We could go for a drive and buy some more colouring books, and have lunch. If it's not too blowy when we come back, we'll walk along the nature trail."

Susie was talking to Miss Blackstock and had hardly touched her cereal.

"Aren't you hungry?"

"Miss Blackstock doesn't like shredded wheat."

"What would she like?"

"Honey crispies."

"Okay. We'll buy some. But let's do some house-cleaning before we leave."

She tidied up, placing the magazines and books in a neat pile on the table, Maclean's volume of Saki on top.

"Tell Miss Blackstock we're ready. We'll go out the front, I'm not going to fight that door every time."

She locked the door after her and stepped on to the beach from the sun-deck. The jetty was deserted, the truck gone. She drove out along Route Six, Maclean's romantic Route Six. She found it hard to believe that this small road winding in and out of the dunes, covered in places with driven sand, rolled on through the entire continent. It was like watching a trickle of water coming from a rock and knowing it was the source of the Nile or the Mississippi.

Two miles short of Orleans she looked in her rear-view

mirror and saw a brown car overtaking her at high speed. The road was narrow and there was traffic approaching ahead. She expected the car to drop in behind her until there was room to pass. Instead, it held speed, drew level and shot past through a gap not much wider than its own body, between Jane's Ford and an oncoming Chevrolet. She saw the terror-stricken face of the Chev's driver and then the brown car was disappearing ahead of her.

"Bloody fool!" she said. The palms of her hands were wet and she slowed down to twenty miles an hour until her nerve returned.

"That was the thin man," Susie said conversationally to her scarf. "There was a thin man and a fat man. Miss Blackstock knows them."

"What thin man?" Jane was still recovering from the narrow escape.

"The thin man at the hotel. He speaks funny."

"You mean the German, Mr. Fischer?"

"The man with hair like wire."

"That wasn't him." She was recalling the frightened face in the Chev. "That was a young man."

"Not in that car, in the brown one."

So now there was a "thin man". They had fled New York because of Susie's "blue man". She had seen another "blue man" and a "red man" on Boylston Street in Boston. Both had been strangers. What if they had all been no more than fantasy-figures? It was not the first time the thought had occurred to her. On the other hand, Walter had said: "I'll follow you. I'll find you." Fantasy or not, she was still pleased she had left New York. And if Susie's "thin man" was, in fact, Willi Fischer, he had nothing to do with Walter: he was part of the ordinary world; an ordinary maniac in a car.

They shopped and had lunch in Chatham and then started back.

"Can we go to the beach now?" Susie asked as they reached the cottage.

76

The wind had freshened, but Jane said: "We can give it a try. I want to change my shoes first."

They walked to the front of the cottage and she noticed that the truck was back in its place on the jetty.

"Put on your anorak," she said.

She changed into a pair of sneakers and was about to follow Susie on to the sun-deck when, glancing around the sitting-room she frowned. Her eyes rested on the coffee-table. The volume of Saki short stories was no longer on top of the magazines as she had left it, but lying at the side.

"Susie, did you move the books?" she called.

Susie came to the door, holding her new colouring book. "No," she replied innocently.

She shrugged. Maybe she had bumped into the table and dislodged it without noticing, or, despite her denial, had actually moved it. Nevertheless, she made sure that both doors were locked before they went out.

She drove to Shoal Point Beach. The moment they stepped out of the car the wind buffeted them and she decided that the nature trail would be more sheltered than the sands. The car park was empty. David Maclean had obviously decided he had done his hospitable duty by her.

The nature reserve lay behind the dunes that ran parallel to the beach. Apart from the man-made path, it was a wilderness area. Within fifty yards of the trail's starting point they might have been a hundred miles from civilisation.

Among the dunes, sheltered from the storms that swept in from the sea, there were plantations of stunted trees: beech, scrub oak and dwarf pine. The leaves were still on the beech and oak trees, crinkled and brown, and they rustled in the wind. This and the noise of the breakers behind the dunes and the occasional cry of a gull were the only sounds; a few litter bins the only evidence of a human hand.

Susie stayed at Jane's side for the first few hundred yards but then, as she grew more used to the place, she skipped ahead as she had the previous day, looking for stones and shells, picking up anything that caught her fancy. It would have been nice, Jane thought, if David had been there. His love-life was no concern of hers, all *she* wanted was companionship.

She had been walking with her head down, kicking the toes of her sneakers into the layers of sand and when she glanced up to check on Susie, the path ahead was empty.

She stopped short, then told herself: she's on the far side of the dune.

"Susie!"

The only answer was the cry of a gull as it passed overhead.

She began to run. Her shoes crunched on the path and her breath was whistling in her windpipe.

She expected to see the child as she reached the other side of the dune, but the landscape was empty of all but the stunted trees and the bending grass and the sand.

Then she heard a human cry, high, blown on the wind. She stopped and held her breath so that her panting would not impair her hearing. The cry came again, from a small valley in the dunes, more heavily bushed than the others, to her right.

She turned off the path and almost immediately she saw, bobbing down the slope towards her, Susie's orange anorak.

She was screaming: "Mummy! Mummy!"

Jane raced towards her and gathered her up in her arms. "What happened?"

Tears were running down the child's cheeks and she was shaking. She clung on to her scarf and thrust one end into her mouth.

"What happened, darling?"

"The blue man."

"Oh, God, where?"

She pointed to the bushed valley.

"Are you sure? Which blue man? The one you saw in Boston, or the one in New York, the one on the steps? Which?"

Susie pointed again. "Blue and red."

"Both?"

78

"No. The blue man, but red here." She indicated her eye.

They had reached the path again and Jane said: "Red here? What do you mean? What was he doing?"

"Sleeping."

"For Heaven's sake, you're not making sense! Susie, listen to me—"

But Susie did not want to listen. She began to cry; aching, racking sobs.

"All right, darling. No more questions. We're going home."

Hand in hand, they half ran, half walked back along the path. Every few steps Jane turned to look over her shoulder. She thought, it *has* become a nervous tic. But knowing made little difference. Even when they came onto the open beach, she still did it.

As they reached the car park she saw David. He was standing with his back to the dunes, staring out to sea through his binoculars. He was dressed in the same blue corduroy wind-cheater he had worn the day before.

Blue wind-cheater! Could he be the blue man Susie had seen? But he could not have reached the beach before her. Unless he had taken a short cut. Wouldn't Susie have recognised him, though?

He turned and smiled. "Hi! I thought you weren't coming." Then he saw the child's tear-marked face and said, "What's up?"

"Susie says she saw a man back there in the dunes."

"And you look as white as a sheet."

"I thought I'd lost her."

He went down on his haunches in front of Susie and said: "What did the man do?"

She looked at him for a long moment, then whispered: "It was the blue man."

"The blue man. I see. Which blue man is that?"

"The blue man and the red man."

He glanced at Jane. "Did he—try anything?"

"I don't think so."

"Did you see him?"

She shook her head.

"Take her back to the cottage, but first tell me where you think she saw him and I'll have a look."

She explained as best she could where Susie had seen the man and he said, "Get on home. I'll look in soon."

She drove back to the cottage. It was mid-afternoon and slate-grey clouds had come up. The wind was whining around the corners of the town. The few people on the sidewalks were huddled into their coats, the fishing-boats were tied up and the harbour was deserted except for the truck on the jetty. The sweetness and charm seemed to have gone out of the place.

David arrived about twenty minutes later. His face was unsmiling. "Can we talk? Just the two of us?"

"I don't want to leave Susie alone."

"Isn't there a TV set in the bedroom? You could keep the door open."

She steered the child back into the other room. In a few moments, she was back. "I found a cartoon programme. She'll be all right for a while. I'll make some coffee."

He waved the suggestion aside. "I think I saw the place you meant. It looked as though there might have been someone lying down there."

She sat on one of the divans and he settled beside her.

"Did you see him?"

"I found—traces."

"What sort of traces?"

There was no smile about his mouth now. "I'll tell you later. First, I think we must stop the guessing games. You're in some sort of trouble, aren't you?"

She automatically rejected the opportunity he was giving her. Over the years of her marriage she had grown so used to keeping her troubles to herself, bottling them up, not even telling her own mother so as not to worry her, that she was out of the habit of offering confidences.

"I'd like to help if I can. I told you I'd noticed your

nervous tic. It's getting worse. If you don't unload some of the stress, it's going to become part of your permanent behaviour pattern.''

"It's pretty ordinary," she said. "A marriage breakup, that's all."

"Ordinary marriages don't end with a nervous wife and a child hiding on the tip of Cape Cod."

The sympathy in his eyes and the cool, unsentimental words breached the wall she had tried to build. There had been no friend in America in whom she had been able to confide. A few brief, unsatisfying telephone calls with her mother and brothers had been her only contact for weeks with anyone close to her. Suddenly, she *wanted* to talk, and once she started, she could not stop. She told him the whole story: about her marriage and divorce, the kidnapping of Susie and the custody battle, Walter's threats, Susie's red and blue men, the incident in Boston, the masked driver on the way to Plymouth, and her current fears. He listened without interruption, though when she was describing Walter's physical attacks on her she saw first a look of disgust, then of anger. "That sort of thing isn't as uncommon as you'd imagine," she said bitterly. "We have shelters for battered wives in England."

Later he said, "I find it hard to associate that kind of violence with civilised people."

"You mean you've always thought of it in terms of Hogarth? The London stews, drunken louts on a Friday night. Believe me, it goes on in the best of families."

"Well . . . now, let's try and make some sense out of what's been happening. After the custody verdict, Hemming came out, down the steps, and said . . . ?"

" 'I'll follow you. I'll find you.' "

"And you think he meant it?"

She raised her hands, then dropped them. "I believe so. I wish I knew for sure. It would be better than this constant uncertainty. He really does want Susie. She belongs to him, you see. Or that's what he feels. I'm not sure he's capable of loving in the way other people understand love. But he's obsessed with possessions. I was one, and so was she. When he was away, he'd call every day and cross-question me about what we'd been doing. It was as though he couldn't bear *his* wife and *his* child having any life apart from him.''

"Why the hell did you marry him?"

"I was on the rebound from someone else. He was different. Dynamic. Get-up-and-go. He was exciting, and at first he spent money as though it was going out of fashion. I was impressed by him and I thought I was in love with him, but even then it was physical rather than emotional. When that wore off, there was nothing.'' She glanced at her watch. She had been talking for an hour.

"For a start, let's dismiss the guy in the hotel in Boston and the one who chased you in his car," David said. "Those were unrelated incidents. Frightening, particularly in your general state of apprehension, but nothing to do with Walter. You're assuming he has been having you followed, intending to grab Susie again, but it seems to me that all you have to go on is her talk about the red and blue men.''

"After she mentioned them the first time I remembered there *was* a man in a blue parka. Walter stood at the top of the steps with him.''

"You're sure they knew each other?"

"Looking back, I seem to have seen them talking to each other.''

"And now you think the man Susie saw in the dunes might have been the same one. Jane, blue parkas out here are as common as grey suits on Madison Avenue.''

Her eyes narrowed. "You said you'd found traces of someone. You haven't told me what they were.''

"I found the place where you and Susie had stood and where she had run down through the sand. I followed her track up to the top of the dune and found other footprints. There was a clump of pine trees and they seemed to circle it. Only there were more steps than one man could have made.''

"Is that all?"

"I found spots of blood on the sand."

"Blood? My God . . . !"

"Hold it. They mightn't mean anything. There was no sign of a man."

"Susie said, 'Red here.' " She touched the side of her face. "That could have been blood."

"It could have been anything. The man might have had a birth mark . . . " He pulled a red handkerchief from the pocket of his wind-cheater and held it to his face. "Say he'd been a hobo, sleeping off a hang-over. He might have put a scarf or a handkerchief like this over his face to shade his eyes. Susie could have woken him and he took himself off."

"What about the blood?"

"He could have cut himself. He may have been injured. He might have had a nose-bleed. It might not even have been his blood. Could have come from an animal."

"It could have been raspberry jam or strawberry ice-cream," she broke in angrily.

"No, it was blood. All I'm trying to do is point out explanations of how it got there."

"You're very rational." She did not believe any of his explanations and she made the word sound like an insult.

"Put it down to my legal training."

They stared at each other. The anger which Jane's fear and confusion had produced was a barrier between them. Then she gathered herself together and said, "I'm sorry. *I'm* being irrational."

"After what you've been through it's amazing that you're so calm. Let's look at things logically. All we have to go on is Susie's word. It was Susie who saw the man on the court-house steps, it was Susie who saw someone through the window of the coffee-shop in New York. But then when you were in Boston she pointed out two other men: just ordinary men, nothing to do with you, one in a blue parka and one in a red parka. Anyway, Walter wasn't wearing a parka, according to you. It was his face that was red. And it was Susie who saw the man on the dune. A 'blue man', asleep, with

83

something red on his face. All I found was disturbed sand, footmarks and some blood—not much, but blood. That's the only ominous thing and there are lots of ways blood-spots could have fallen on the sand.''

''Then why did Susie come haring down in such a state?''

''Maybe she came upon him unexpectedly and got a fright.''

''And what about Walter's threats?''

''People say things in the heat of the moment, especially when they've lost a fight. He was humiliated because you'd been awarded custody. He was angry. He made threats. Maybe he never intended to carry them out.''

''You don't know Walter.''

''I've known others like him.''

''So what's all this leading to?''

''I'm suggesting that all we have to go on is Susie's word, and that might not be entirely reliable. You're her mother, so you're not in the best spot to be objective. Would you say she was imaginative?''

''She makes up stories. But so do most children'''

''What about that scarf? I've heard her talking to it as though it was alive.''

''Children often relate to improbable objects.''

''But she has her own world of the imagination, doesn't she? A world of her own. Does it bother you?''

''Why should it?''

''Doesn't she cut you out at times? Couldn't it be that your experiences with Walter have made *you* over-possessive? So you try to force yourself into her world by accepting the situations she creates.''

''For God's sake!'' she said. ''What the hell gives you the right to play parlour psychologist?''

He stiffened. ''I'm sorry. So it's none of my goddam business, right?''

Her anger dissipated as quickly as it had formed and she made a despairing gesture. ''Oh, I suppose you could be right. Maybe I'm so scared of losing her that I've lost all sense of proportion. Sometimes I've even thought that Walter wants to put on so much pressure that I'd crack. If anything happened to me, he'd get her, you see. I suppose that's ridiculous, isn't it?''

To her surprise, he shook his head. ''Maybe not. Having a man follow you in London was clearly his way of creating tension. But he can only achieve anything if you let him get to you.''

She stood up and found he had been holding her hand.

''Where are you going?''

''To look at Susie.''

''You put her in the bedroom. You switched on the TV. The door's open. There's no way she could have got out without being seen by us. You see what I mean about that nervous tic?''

She stopped and smiled wryly. ''Perhaps Susie and I *could* have created this situation out of our imaginations. Anyway, you've made me feel better and I thank you for that. I hope you're right. But I just wish we were back in England.''

''I'm glad you're not. Especially as we're about to celebrate your new peace of mind with a drink. Is there any of that Canadian Club left? We could do with one.''

''Two,'' she said. ''I hadn't realised soul-baring was such thirsty work.''

When she brought his drink he patted the divan beside him and she sat down. He recaptured her hand and studied it.

''Skål,'' he said. ''And you have beautiful hands.''

''My mother used to say I should have been a pianist.''

''Not so. Pianists need powerful hands, plenty of muscle. Yours are ladies' hands, long--fingered, slender, well-kept nails.''

''It's the luxury of living in hotels, not having had to do any washing-up or housework.''

''Okay . . . now to revert to the subject under discussion. Assuming that imagination has been the major cause of your apprehensions, what are we left with?''

85

"You tell me."

"We're left with phantoms. If we went to the police about Susie's story, they'd laugh at us."

"Have you been laughing at *me*?"

"Far from it."

"Well, what do I do now?"

"Stay close."

"To what?"

"To me, and let me look after you for the rest of the week."

"I meant, shouldn't I fly home from New York without wasting any more time?"

"No," he said firmly. "We might have killed your dragons, but you look as though you've just come out of gaol. Dr. Maclean prescribes rest, relaxation, good food and drink. Mostly with him."

"That sounds nice," she admitted.

"Stay in tonight. I have to go back now, but I'll come over in a little while. I'll bring something from the kitchen and we'll have a picnic."

"Okay, doctor."

After he had gone, a thought came to her: what was he proposing to do with his lady friend during her rest-cure? She found she didn't much care, as long as she had his reassuring company.

But it was not so easy to cling to his reassurance when she was alone. Her nightmares hurried back. She wanted to believe he was right, that what she was afraid of were only phantoms created in her mind. Maybe, if she stopped looking over her shoulder, they would no longer exist.

She gazed out of her window at the darkening harbour and the gusting wind. It was a desolate scene. She shivered as a few lines from Coleridge came into her mind.

> *Like one that on a lonesome road*
> *Doth walk in fear and dread*
> *And having once turned round walks on,*

And turns no more his head;
Because he knows, a frightful fiend
Doth close behind him tread.

She closed the blinds and put on the lights. She picked up her book of Saki's short stories, looking forward to David's return.

She read 'The Unrest Cure' and 'The Pipes of Pan' and one or two more. It was dark when she decided to wake Susie, and went into the bedroom. The Boston weatherman was on TV with a huge chart. "And in the Massachusetts Bay area, high winds and rain tonight. There'll be storms tomorrow but maybe, *maybe* there'll be some sunshine too." He drew a big question-mark on the chart. She stood by the bed, amused at the production number he made out of the weather, thinking how staid British television was by comparison. "R-A-I-N!" he yelled, swooping again at the chart. "That's what's on the way. And then some *real* cold weather." He wrote "WOW" under arrows down from Siberia and Canada.

She switched off, woke Susie and held her for a few moments while she came to full consciousness.

"How about an omelette for supper?" she said.

Susie shook her head.

"A boiled egg?"

"No."

It was amazing how much conversation it took to determine each of Susie's meals.

"Scrambled eggs?"

"No!"

"No, *thank you*. What do you want?"

"Aren't we going to the hotel?"

"I'm going to give you your supper here tonight."

There was a knock on the street door and her spirits lifted. "That's David. Maybe he's brought something nice for you."

"I like David."

She went to the warped door, wondering why he had come that way. She unlocked it and tugged, but it would not budge. "Push," she called.

It flew open. It was not David who stood in the light, but the bearded figure of Peter Davidson.

"Sorry to bother you, but I wanted to know if you were coming over for dinner. It's a lousy night and we're closing early."

"David . . . Mr. Maclean said he was . . . "

"He's not here. He went out a while back. Said he was going to Hyannis. I'd be happy for you to come over. I'd enjoy your company."

He smiled and instantly looked years younger. She realised he was more attractive than at first he had appeared. Without his white tunic, wearing grey slacks and a heather-mixture sweater, he looked more like a member of the local art-colony than a cook—certainly more so than Pate and Fischer. She hesitated as she absorbed what he had said. David had let her down again. He had told her he would return in a little while and then, without even a message, had left for Hyannis. It would take him hours to drive there and back. Whatever urgent business had come up, at least he could let her know. With rising anger, she decided that she was not going to hang about and wait for him.

"We'll be right there," she said briskly.

"Are you ready now? I'll walk you over."

The hotel wore a sad and abandoned look, with no one behind the bar and no one in front of it. The tables were laid in the restaurant, but there were no customers. Peter took them to their usual table and said; "I haven't put on a special tonight. Didn't seem worth it. But there's clam chowder and lobster . . . "

"Could you do me a steak?"

"Sure. What about Susie? More sausages?"

"I want scrambled eggs, please."

"You got 'em."

Jane sighed. "She refused my scrambled eggs a few

minutes ago. What's the secret of your success?"

He grinned. "Either I'm a better cook than you or I have the charm of novelty."

After he had brought their meal he returned to the kitchen. The restaurant was so silent Jane found herself whispering to Susie, hoping someone would come in: Fischer, Pate, even da Souza; anyone to cheer the place up.

Peter appeared. "Anything else?" She shook her head. "Have some coffee. I feel bad about rushing you."

"All right. Thank you."

He brought her a cup, and hovered.

"Did David tell you when he'd be back?" she asked.

"David doesn't tell me anything." There it was again, the hostility she had noticed when she had first arrived. Had he also suffered from Maclean's irresponsibility? She sensed an unwillingness to answer questions, but she was curious. Her irritation at David's failure to reappear had been growing throughout the meal. Clearly, his frequent solicitude and sympathy had been no more than a façade. And yet, he had seemed so genuine . . .

"Have you known him long?" she said.

"No."

"I understand he was a lawyer."

"Yes."

"I wonder what brought him out here?"

"I wouldn't know."

"Doesn't it seem odd that he would buy a place like this, with no training in hotel work?"

He shrugged and said nothing.

She gave up and changed the subject. "How about you? Do you like it here? It must be lonely in winter."

"It's the best time. I've seen the streets so crowded in summer you can hardly move."

He wiped the table with a cloth. Reluctant to return to the lonely cottage so early, she said, "Won't you have a drink with me?"

"Well, okay, thanks. I'll have a beer."

When he came back he had taken off his white tunic. He sat down at the table. "Are you from this area?" she said.

"Detroit. Ever been there?"

"No."

"If you had, you wouldn't ask if I liked it here. This is paradise compared with Detroit."

They laughed together, then she said, "What do you do with your spare time in winter?"

"Did you happen to notice the paintings in the lobby?"

"Yours? They're marvellous. I saw them the day I arrived."

"I've had two exhibitions, one in Provincetown, one in New Bedford. Can't make a living from painting, though."

"Is that why you came here in the first place, to paint?"

He nodded. 'I love painting the dunes." Enthusiasm had made his face brighten. She found herself warming to him and enjoying a conversation she had started only to pass the time. Though lacking David's intelligence, he was easy, undemanding company—and probably a whole lot more reliable, too, she thought, irritably. "I like to go driving in the dunes," he was saying. "I've got a VW dune-buggy. It's great."

"I've never been in one."

"I'll take you some time. It's better than a roller-coaster."

"I'd like that. Have you ever seen any of Mr. Fischer's work. He paints, too, doesn't he?"

He made a disbelieving face. "So I'm told. I haven't seen any evidence of it. We get a load of 'would-bes' like him here —would-be painters, writers, what-have-you. Mostly they don't do a damn thing."

"I gather he lives with Mr. Pate."

"The so-called writer? Yeah. They share a house up the road."

"You don't care for them?"

"They're a couple of old . . . " He glanced at Susie. "You know what I mean. This place has its fair share of them, too."

There was silence for a moment, then she said: "Is David a good pupil?"

"Pupil?"

"I gather you're helping him to learn the hotel business."

He shrugged. "He's okay, only like I said, you got to be flexible in this business. A guy came last night, late. He wanted to stay. There's a little room with a bunk bed downstairs that Bill Dugan sometimes rented out of season. But David said no. Where the hell else is a guy going to find a bed in this place at that time of night? Do him a favour, he would have told his friends, maybe come back himself. See what I mean?"

Before she could stop herself, she said: "What did he look like? What was he wearing?"

"Who?"

"The man who wanted a room."

"I only saw the back of his head through the kitchen hatch. I heard them talking. Why?"

"Nothing." She saw him look at her oddly. It was stupid to go on like this. But what if he *had* been wearing a blue parka?

Peter finished his beer and stood up. "It's always the same," he said, with sudden bitterness. "I could turn this place into a gold-mine. Good food, good service, open all year. I'd work round the clock in summer, have time to paint in the winter. But I haven't got the money to buy it. *He* had the money, but he doesn't know how to run it. He doesn't know what hard work is. Doesn't want to be bothered. Spends all his time watching goddam birds."

"I'm sorry," she said. "Maybe some day . . . "

"It's always maybe. Always some day."

"You'll have other exhibitions."

"I guess so. Well, I got to clear up. Nice talking to you. Perhaps we can get together again before you leave."

"I'd like that."

She was in bed by ten o'clock, trying and failing to concentrate on a thriller in which an improbable Englishman saves the world from nuclear holocaust. Why had David not come back? If he was tied up he could at least have sent a message. Was it the lady friend? Maybe she'd had her own plans for the evening, which didn't include Jane. She told herself she was suffering from hurt pride, but that didn't help. She had enjoyed his company and had been looking forward to seeing him again. He had seemed genuinely absorbed in her problems but clearly it had been superficial, and she found herself regretting her frankness.

She forced her mind away from him to Peter Davidson. He was an interesting character. Painter, chef, table-waiter, a man with considerable bitterness festering inside him. She now recognised the roots of his hostility towards Maclean; it was the old enemy, envy.

She fell asleep, still thinking about the two men, and awoke a little after two in the morning. It was an instant awakening: heart pounding, skin crawling, ears straining. Then she heard the noise that had woken her, a kind of scraping at the street door, as though someone was trying to push it open. She could not remember locking it. It came again, a soft, scuffling, grating sound. Was that the door moving? She flung back her covers and tiptoed towards it, fumbled for the light switch and flicked it on.

The door was locked and the chain was up. In the same seconds, she heard footsteps on the sidewalk outside, hurrying away.

An envelope was lying just inside the door. She ripped it open and read: "Sorry about tonight, but the picnic's only postponed, not cancelled—I hope. Please forgive me. D."

She felt a mixture of irritation and, despite herself, pleasure that he had bothered to write; at least that was something. She returned to bed feeling happier, not only because of the note, but because those hurried footsteps in the dark had been David's and not . . . not whose?

6

The Boston weatherman had been right. The next day started well, clear and cold with brilliant sunshine, but Jane could see a bank of dark cloud on the horizon. Nonetheless, it was a day for being outside. She wondered whether David would call and was conscious of listening for the telephone as she and Susie had breakfast. It did not ring.

Again she felt let down. Well, she was not going to sit waiting for him. If he wanted to see her, he could find her.

There were one or two items of shopping she needed, presents for her brothers and a memento of Cape Cod for her mother, so at ten o'clock she and Susie emerged into the bright street. The little town, its white houses gleaming in the sunshine, had regained much of its charm.

She said to Susie: ''We'll walk up the hill and buy some postcards, and then . . . ''

''Good morning, Mrs. Hemming! Lovely day, isn't it?'' She turned and saw Dennis Pate's plump figure behind her. ''I wonder if you would do me the honour of allowing me to give you a cup of coffee? Not coffee for you, of course, my dear.'' He smiled down at Susie. ''Something nicer than that. Or don't you like ice-cream? Perhaps it's too soon after breakfast.'' It was a compelling, dimpled smile and Susie smiled back tentatively.

Jane smiled, too. He made her think of Sidney Greenstreet in the old movies, and he looked even stouter in a black leather coat and a black Beatles' cap.

''It appears that Susie does like ice-cream.'' He bent towards her again. ''To tell you a secret, so do I! And that's

93

why I'm not as thin as I should be. What do you say, Mrs. Hemming? I think I have one taker, what about you?"

"A cup of coffee would be nice."

"Good, good! This way then." He led them along a narrow lane and up some steps. They came out near the top of the low hill on which Margate was partly built, where she had parked her car on first arriving.

She found that Pate was not guiding her to a coffee-shop, for he led her through a gate to a large wooden house which had been painted pale yellow. He unlocked the front door and stood aside with a courtly bow. "Come in out of the cold."

She hesitated and, as though reading her mind, he said: "My coffee is ten times better than you'll get anywhere else in this town."

The house was furnished in light pine and seemed to comprise a middle section consisting of a large, open-plan living-room and kitchen, with a suite on either side containing bedrooms and bathrooms.

"This is very pleasant," she said.

"I prefer something a little cosier, dear, but for a rented house it isn't bad, and the view is gorgeous." He turned to Susie. "Now, what's it going to be? We can do you a banana split or a hot fudge sundae or a pêche Melba or . . . " She chose the banana split.

"Splendid. And you can help me." He took her hand and they moved around a breakfast bar into the kitchen. Jane followed and saw the happy anticipation on her daughter's face. This is what she needs, she thought: other people to make a fuss of her, to take her out of herself and out of the claustrophobic life she's been leading in hotel rooms.

"But first of all, let me give your mother her coffee. How do you like it?"

"Black. No sugar."

"As it should be drunk." He poured her a cup from an expensive Italian automatic filter that stood on the bar. "I think you'll like that. I have it made up to my own blending: Java for smoothness and crisp Colombian so it isn't too bland. But now for the most important person." He deftly concocted a banana split from two kinds of ice-cream and bananas, topped with raspberry jam, a dollop of cream and chopped nuts. As he handed it to the child Jane saw him look at it longingly.

"There," he said. "Let's take it and sit by the window."

She had been looking around the room, which was Scandinavian in its simplicity. "I don't see any of Mr. Fischer's paintings," she remarked.

"He keeps them in his studio. "It's a couple of blocks away."

"But you do your writing here?"

"My writing? My dear, I only need a typewriter and a few sheets of paper for that. My desk is in there." He nodded to the right-hand suite.

"How is your book going?"

"Not badly, but let's not talk about Aubrey on a sunny morning like this. That's the darker side of life. I think life does rather fall into one side or the other, don't you, the dark and the light? Rather like beer. Dunkles und helles." He gave a little, dimpled giggle.

It was a cliché that women felt at home with homosexuals, but true for all that. She found herself enjoying his somewhat malicious gossip and the lack of sexual tension.

After a while he leant forward and said cosily. "And how do you like us?" She hesitated. "I mean the town. Do you find the natives friendly?"

"I haven't met many, but yes, I do, except . . ."

"Yes?"

"Oh, nothing, really. We had a bad start. The first person we spoke to here was a woman who was—not rude, exactly, but unwelcoming. She was in the pharmacy when we went in to ask directions to the hotel. There was a kind of . . . of hostility. Or perhaps it was just my imagination. We'd been driving all day and we were tired."

"Can't have been a local," Pate said. "They like strangers in winter. Cheers the place up a bit. What did she look like?"

Jane described the woman in the grey suede coat and boots. There was a pause as she waited for him to react, then he said: "No, I can't say it rings any bell. She must have been a visitor."

"She knew about the Fisherman's Arms."

Dismissing the subject, he turned to Susie. "What's the verdict? Good?"

"Yes, thank you."

"Have you ever seen one of these?" He took from his pocket a small electronic game with moving figures which fell down manholes unless the operator was able to cover them in time by pressing the right buttons. He explained its principles and Susie began to play with it.

"She's a lovely little girl," he said to Jane. "But it must be lonely for her."

"Lonely?"

"Travelling the way you do."

"We don't travel all the time, and we're going home soon."

"So it's a holiday?"

"At the moment." He was looking at her expectantly and she felt impelled to add: "I was in New York on . . . on business. Then we went to Boston and couldn't get a flight for a week, so we came out here."

"What kind of business was that?"

"Family business."

"I'm glad to hear it. You look too young and pretty to be a career girl."

"Come now, Mr. Pate . . . "

"Dennis, dear."

"I wouldn't have guessed you were a male chauvinist!"

"Well, hardly. It's just that career girls frighten me. They're so *efficient*. What about Mr. Hemming? Did you leave him behind in Boston?"

"I'm divorced."

"That must make your life difficult."

"It was more difficult being married."

He sighed. "Sometimes one wondered what one was missing. One would be filled with regret. But on the whole, I don't think I'm sorry I'm not married." He turned to watch Susie. "The one thing I'm really sad about is that I have no children. Bachelors can be lonely people, you know." He warmed to his own self-pity. "I've always been very fond of children. Very fond. And I think they know that. Susie, would you like to keep that game?"

"Oh, no!" Jane said. "They're very expensive."

"Allow me my pleasure. I assure you, it's a totally selfish gesture." Reluctantly, she gave in, and he patted her arm.

A few minutes later he saw them to the door. As Jane thanked him he said, "Perhaps you will let me take Susie out one day. It would give you a bit of a break."

"I don't think . . ."

"It can't have been much fun for you lately, dear. What you need is a little time to yourself."

"Perhaps some time. I'm sure Susie would enjoy it."

As she walked down the hill into town she decided that Pate was a perceptive man. He had been right. She did need time to herself, time to think out her future; she needed a break, however brief, from her concentration on Susie, for both their sakes.

There was a car parked outside her cottage and as they drew nearer she saw it was David's, but it was empty. They walked towards it and she found herself reluctant to face him. Last night, even this morning, she had been angry with him. He *had* taken the trouble to leave her a note, but was she expected to ignore the fact that he had let her down?

She still had not made up her mind what attitude to adopt when Susie said, "There's David." She was pointing down a narrow side street. He was standing outside a white frame house, talking to a woman. Susie dashed towards them and Jane followed, calling her back. She took no notice.

When Jane was a few yards short of them Susie had already reached David's side and was holding up her new game for him to admire. Jane glanced at the woman, who was watching from the doorway, and stopped short. It was the elegant foreigner from the pharmacy and her expression, as Susie claimed David's attention, was cold. She was in her early forties, greyhound slim with high cheekbones and long dark hair drawn back from her face into a roll at the nape of her neck; wearing lizard-skin pumps, a soft crimson mohair skirt cinched at her small waist with a wide suede belt, a cashmere sweater. All very, very expensive. Even seeing her from a distance made Jane feel ill-dressed and overweight.

The woman gave her no chance to speak. As she drew level with them Jane heard her say hurriedly to David: "I see you again soon." She stepped back inside and closed the door.

"Hullo, I've been hunting all over town for you," he said, and she thought he looked discomfited.

"I was out."

"I'd managed to work that out for myself." He fell into step beside her as she turned towards the cottage. "We have things to talk about."

"Have we?"

"Yes, we have. Or I have. I couldn't come back last night, and I couldn't let you know. Something urgent came up that I had to deal with. I can only apologise."

She glanced at the house they had just left. "Something to do with the hotel?"

"Not exactly." He grinned. "But not what you're thinking."

"She's very attractive. What's her name?"

"Stephanie Hirsch. She's Swiss."

She waited for something more, a clue to their relationship, but he offered none. He didn't owe her any explanations, she thought, and was angry with herself for letting the situation irritate her. She smiled and said, "Thank you for your note."

"I didn't call you earlier this morning because I've been out since seven, collecting wood."

"What for?"

"Our picnic, of course. Where have you been?"

"With a gentleman friend."

"What gentleman friend?" A frown crossed his face and she felt a flush of pleasure. He recovered and said: "Tell me who he is and I'll knock his head off."

"Are you asking me to be indiscreet?" she said lightly. "You tell me about the beautiful Madame Hirsch and I'll tell you about my gentleman friend."

"I hardly know her." There was irritation in his voice.

"Does she live in Margate?"

"For part of the year."

"Is there a Mr. Hirsch?"

"Presumably. How should I know? Now, are we ready for that picnic?"

"Of course. Where are we going?"

"You'll see."

Susie sat on the front seat between them. There were rugs and a big hamper in the back.

They drove out of town, forked right and went on down the coast. At first there was constraint between them, and Jane sensed that he had resented her questions.

It was forgotten when, after driving for twenty minutes, they came through the dunes to Shoal Point, near the lighthouse. He pulled into an empty parking-lot, its spaces marked in white lines which had been faded by the summer sun, then sifted over by a thin layer of sand. Jane looked around. There was a small, wooden-framed restaurant with a 'closed' notice hanging crookedly in a window; at the far end of the lot, a pay phone, its glazed panels rimed with salt and sand. That was all. There was the sadness of summer's ending about the place, and yet it had its own charm, even with the looming black clouds that were building up on the horizon. Deserted, it had a wild beauty that would be invisible when it was invaded by the summer hordes.

They walked down on to the long beach which they could see from end to end. The sea was rolling in, the breakers white-tipped, yellowish as they ran up the sand, grey-black further out where the clouds were reflected in the tossing water.

The wind was fresh, the air the crisp cold of a mountain stream, exhilarating and refreshing. Jane felt a surge of pure pleasure such as she had not experienced for years. The mysterious man who had frightened Susie in the dunes, the masked driver, the arrogant Swiss woman, even Walter, seemed to disappear down the wrong end of a telescope. Her mood must have communicated itself to David, for when Susie saw a pyramid of driftwood and cried, "We're going to have a bonfire!" he picked her up and swung her in a circle, saying, "We certainly are! If that storm will hold off for a couple of hours, we're going to have the best bonfire you ever saw."

He poured kerosene over the kindling and lit it, then fetched the picnic basket from the car and spread the rugs. He peered into the hamper. "There are hamburgers and frankfurters and steaks. I guess it's usual to have a clambake on the beach, but I want something more filling when it's cold."

"So do I." Jane rubbed her hands together and held them out to the fire.

"And how about this?" He held up an icy bottle wrapped in aluminium foil. "Genuine, California-style Riesling."

They stood around the flames, drinking the white wine. When the fire had burned down to manageable proportions, he raked some embers to the side and began to barbecue the meat. They ate in the vast silence of the beach, listening to the surf and the crackling of the wood.

When they had finished, Susie went shell-collecting and they built up the fire and sat warming themselves and sipping their wine. Jane said, "I haven't enjoyed myself so much for a long time."

"That's because it's simple. Most simple things are best."

She thought of Walter, to whom simple pleasures were synonymous with boredom. Throughout their marriage, they had never gone on a picnic, walked on a beach, sat by a fire listening to the ocean. She wondered, now, how she could have endured the endless expense-account meals, the restless seeking after amusement, the so-called friends, driven by ambition and money-hunger. She looked down at her jeans and thick, loose sweater and thought, without regret, of the spectacular dresses, a legacy from her marriage, that hung, unworn, in her wardrobe at home. So this is the real me, she thought, wryly: a simple soul made for simple pleasures with a . . . she glanced at David . . . far from simple man. She warmed herself with the memory of his remark as they had reached the beach: "Thank God you're not the kind of woman who turns up at a picnic in high heels and flowing skirts. You look exactly right—and sexy with it!"

After a brief silence he said, "I want to show you something."

He pulled her to her feet and, catching her quick look at Susie, he said, "She'll be all right. There's no one around for miles."

They walked through the sand, parallel with the parking-lot and she saw, on the side of a dune, half-buried by drift-sand, the ruins of a house. It must once have been beautiful, but was now only a shell, a frame building on wooden piles. Sand had filled in the area underneath it and the back rooms had been almost engulfed. The windows were long gone and only the sea-facing rooms, with the remains of a sun-deck in front of them, still had protection against the weather. The sun had disappeared and the storm clouds had built into a great black mountain range towering over the land. The house stood, skeletal against the sand and, as they stepped onto the deck, Jane could hear its timbers creaking in the wind. She found herself half-fascinated, half-repelled by its atmosphere.

"It's eerie. Who lived here?" she said.

"An old man from Boston, I understand. Imagine how lonely it must have been. He and his family used to come for the summers. Then his wife and children were killed in a fire in Portland, Maine, and he spent the last twenty years of his life alone here."

"And then?"

"After he died, with nobody to leave it to, it fell into ruins. I like to come here. It's so remote from the real world."

They walked up the side of the dune and he pulled her up on to the verandah.

Holding hands, they went through what had once been French windows into a big room. Half the ceiling had collapsed and they could see the stormy sky through the roof, from which several tiles were missing.

"Careful!" David said, as she stepped on a rotting floorboard that began to splinter under her weight. "They put up a notice during the summer warning people the place is dangerous, but it disappeared. I suppose some kid took it as a souvenir."

Cautiously testing each board, she made her way through the house, peering into the collapsing rooms, with their reminders that this had once been someone's home: the strips of wall-paper flapping in the wind; the marks on the walls where shelves had once been; the empty pipes protruding into what must have been the kitchen; the holes where bathroom fittings had been wrenched away; the doors, hanging from broken, rusty hinges, from which the weather had stripped all the paint.

"One day it'll all be gone," David said. "The dunes will take it back."

She shivered. "Let's go outside again. It gives me the creeps."

They stepped into the big, ruined living-room, and he kissed her. She realised she had been waiting for it. They stood in the deserted house and she put her arms around his neck. The kiss developed by stages until there was something savage about it, as though they were trying to overpower each other with their lips and tongues. She felt him hard against her, one hand in the small of her back, pulling her towards him. Off-balance, she struggled. He supported her as she was borne down to the floor, his hands on her body.

She pulled away. "No!"

"Why not?"

"Not here. Not now."

"Susie's all right, for God's sake!"

"It's not Susie." She rolled away from him and stood up. How could she explain about Walter, how could she tell him that this was where Walter would have wanted her, here on the sandy floor or against one of the walls, on the top of a dune? And then there was the Hirsch woman. Had David brought her here, as well?

She said, "It isn't you," and put her hand out to touch his cheek.

"Why, then?" At first he had seemed angry but now, he just looked embarrassed.

"Just say I'm a lady who is built for comfort, not for speed."

The beginnings of a smile touched his lips. "You mean, you're for it in principle?"

"Yes. But the timing's bad and the place is—sad."

"Another time?"

"Another time. A rain check."

"And for now? Friends?"

"Of course."

They stood on the edge of the deck. The air cut like a knife and the sky was darkening. Sheet lightning lit the horizon and there was a distant rumble of thunder. The storm would soon be on them, Jane thought, but she was reluctant to end the day. David had taken her hand again and was holding it in the warmth of his pocket. She glanced towards the ashes of their fire and saw that Susie had not stirred.

"Were you ever married?" she said suddenly.

His angular face closed. "In another life. Or that's the way it seems."

"What happened?"

"She died."

"I'm sorry. I'd assumed . . ."

"There are other ways of ending a marriage than divorce."

"Yes. Children?"

"None. We'd planned to have three. She was killed in a road accident in New Jersey."

103

"Were you . . . ?" She stopped.

"No. I wasn't driving. Her mother was. She shouldn't have been, but she loved driving. A seventy-four year old lady with cataracts in both eyes. They hit a tree. No traffic, no other cars involved. They just hit a tree and that was the end of it."

"Both of them?"

"Both of them."

She put her hand out and touched his cheek. "I'm so sorry."

"Let's go back to the fire. You must be cold. I guess we'd better pack up and get away before the storm breaks." He turned her towards him and put his hands on her shoulders. "You meant that? About a rain-check?"

She nodded.

"In that case, let's work off our libido before we go home. The English take cold showers and play hockey, don't they? We'll run. See that tree-trunk in the water?" He pointed to a log that rolled on the edge of the waves about half a mile along the beach. "I'll race you there."

"I told you I was built for comfort . . ."

"It'll do you good. I'll give you twenty seconds start. Now go! One . . . two . . . three . . . four . . ."

She jumped into the loose sand and began ploughing her way along the beach.

"Hurry up!" he shouted. "It's going to rain in a minute."

"You didn't count to twenty."

"I gave you thirty."

She was on hard, wet sand now and heard the slap-slap of her feet and felt the spray soak through her sneakers.

"Hey, you look great!" he called. "I've got a thing about ladies' bottoms in jeans."

She laughed and slowed down, panting. "I can't go on."

He caught up with her. "You nearly made it."

The dark shape of the log was about twenty yards away and it was then, as they looked closely at it for the first time, she realised that there was something wrong: the log was not a log.

"Jesus!" David said.

She gripped his arm and they ran forward together.

The log was the body of a man. It lay half in and half out of the water and each time the surf hissed up the beach it moved the legs so that they looked alive. The man lay on his stomach. He was dressed in a pair of checked trousers and a dark grey shirt. His feet were bare and there were purple marks on his ankles.

"Don't come any further," David said.

He knelt beside the body and put his hand on the chest.

"Dead?" She already knew the answer.

"Yes." He caught the body under the arms and dragged it up the beach. She went forward and he said, "Wait!" But it was too late. She saw the man's face. The top and side of his head had been smashed in as though he had fallen from a cliff. His left eye was missing. He was a stranger to her, but she felt her gorge rise.

"Get hold of yourself!" David said. "Go back for Susie. I'm going to call the police."

As he disappeared over a dune on his way to the pay phone in the parking-lot, she ran towards Susie, who was still lying, asleep, warm and protected under her rug, though big drops of rain were falling.

Jane woke her gently then, keeping her voice level with an effort, said: "Come on, darling, we're going back to the car."

Susie yawned, then said, "Can I look for some more shells first?"

"No! We must hurry or we'll get wet. Bring your rug. We'll leave everything else."

"Where's David?"

"He's already gone to the car."

As she spoke, a mixture of hail and rain began to lash the beach. The stinging drops were icy and, as she dragged Susie over the dunes, thunder and lightning were almost simultaneous overhead.

"Run, Susie!"

Momentarily, her need to get away from the place was swamped by the necessity to find shelter. Almost without conscious thought, she made for the ruined house. She heaved Susie up onto the wooden verandah, then pulled her into the inadequate shelter of the front room.

They huddled together under a section of more or less undamaged roof and watched the storm gather fury. The sky had become so dark it might have been dusk and they had to shout to make themselves heard above the rain and the thunder.

As the hammering of Jane's heart subsided, she became aware of a smell: not of wet sand and vegetation as she would expect; a curious, rancid, winey smell which she had certainly not noticed before in the house. She was still sniffing, wondering what it was, when, as suddenly as it had started, the rain diminished. From a hammering, it became a gentle patter, and she and Susie could use their normal voices again.

"Can we go to the car now?" Susie said.

"Let's wait a moment and make sure . . . "

A floor-board creaked. She swung around and peered into the depths of the house. It came again, the same noise she had made when she had stepped on the splitting floorboard and David had warned her to be careful. Was someone else in the house?

"David?" she said. "Is that you?"

There was no answer. She stood absolutely still, only her eyes moving from side to side, trying to penetrate the darkness. There was a sound like a nail being drawn over rusty metal—or someone making a door move against its ancient hinges.

There was a presence all around her. Almost as though a hand was reaching out for her, she could *feel* someone was watching them.

She felt for Susie's hand, but no small fist buried itself in hers, and she looked down. She was alone in the room. "Susie?" she whispered.

There was no answer and she began to grope her way

towards a narrow doorway which seemed to lead to a walk-in closet. Its door was half off its hinges. "Susie?" The closet was dark. She reached out, like a blind woman, and, at shoulder-height, she touched something warm, that moved. Clothing. The sour smell was suddenly stronger. She stumbled back.

"Susie!" This time it was a scream, a roof-raising cry of terror that drowned the last rumblings of the storm and echoed through the old house.

From her left, outside the room, she heard a call: "Mummy!" and a crash. Careless of danger, she ran across the uneven floor. She found Susie in what had once been a hall. She had put her foot through a gap and slipped down between two floorboards. But she was not hurt and as Jane reached her, she was already hauling herself up. Jane was helping her when she heard the sounds again: the creaking, the door grating on its hinge. Still holding the child, she turned and there, in the doorway, she saw the figure of a man, watching her. It was too dark to make out his features, but as she stood, rigid, her eyes wide, he began to move and she heard his hoarse breathing.

"Jane!" David's call came from the verandah. "Where the hell are you?"

In an instant, the man had disappeared.

"David!"

"For God's sake, what are you doing here?"

Clutching Susie, she ran to him and his arms went around them both.

"There was a man . . . " she stammered. "In the cupboard . . . he was watching us . . . "

"There isn't anyone for miles," he said. "You must have seen a shadow."

"But . . . "

She stopped as they heard the sound of a car's engine, coming from the opposite direction to the parking lot. "There *was* someone," she said quietly.

7

Chief Boyd was a man of medium height with blue eyes surrounded by pale lashes. He was going bald, but instead of allowing the wisps of blond hair to lie across his sunburnt skull, he'd had it cut short so that it stood up in bristles. He was broad-shouldered, now, in middle age, running to fat. But he looked hard and tough and, with his Nordic complexion, reminded Jane of German panzer officers she had seen in old movies.

On the other side of the glass partition of his office, two patrolmen worked at their desks, one writing and one typing. A radio call-sign chattered in the distance.

"Goddam it!" Boyd said, swinging left and right in his swivel chair. "Goddam it, why now? Why on my beach!"

The body had been collected and taken to Boston for an autopsy and identification. David was still at the beach, helping Boyd's men search the tide-line for anything that might have been washed up with the corpse.

He was grumbling about being short-handed in winter, and Christmas coming on, but most of Jane's attention was given to wondering if Susie was all right. She had not wanted to desert her, but even less had she wanted to bring her. She had been able to think of no one to leave her with except Dennis Pate, so before obeying Boyd's summons she had hurried to his house and rung the bell. She had heard voices and then the door had opened and she had caught a glimpse of a figure swiftly crossing the main room, a flash of red disappearing through a doorway on the left. She had the impression, even in the half darkness, that it was a woman.

For a moment, there had been no welcoming smile on Pate's face, then he said: "Well, this *is* a pleasant surprise. Hullo, Susie."

Jane spoke swiftly: "I'm sorry to bother you, but I have to go and see the police. David Maclean and I found a body washed up on the beach at Shoal Point."

Again his smile had disappeared and his pouched eyes widened: "A body? At Shoal Point?"

"I don't want Susie with me. Could you entertain her for a while? I can't think of anywhere else to take her."

He did not reply at once and she had been afraid he was going to refuse, then he said: "My dear, I would have been insulted if you hadn't come to me. Here I am, all by myself, wondering how to spend the evening. It's not quite the cocktail hour and we old bachelors get lonely at this time of day." He held out a hand to Susie. "Come on, darling, and we'll see if we can find you a marzipan mouse."

She went to him willingly and as Jane turned to leave he had said: "A body! What a shock. We'll have a drink together when you fetch her and you must tell me all about it. I'm longing to hear."

Now, in Boyd's office, she was gnawing at the quick around one of her nails. The interrogation had taken much longer than she had anticipated. She was uneasy about Susie. Why had Pate lied about being alone? Who was the woman she had seen? Could it have been Willi Fischer in drag? That would explain Pate's secretiveness.

A stenographer came in to take her statement. "You can sign it tomorrow when it's been typed," the Chief told her.

For the next twenty minutes, everything but the problem of producing a coherent statement went out of her mind and it was nearly seven o'clock by the time she had finished.

She hurried through the cold, empty streets. When she rang Pate's bell, she heard soft chimes, but no one came. She rang again. Still no answer. She opened the letter flap and peered through. There was a light on inside and she heard voices. She could not make out what was being said, but she recognised Pate's high voice, then the tones of a woman. They seemed to be arguing. There was a third voice, rougher and deeper. She banged on the door with the brass knocker, ringing the bell simultaneously. Instantly, the voices ceased. A moment later, Pate opened the door. He was flushed and stared at her briefly as though he did not recognise her. "Jane, my dear! Uh . . . Susie's watching television. I'll call her." There was no further mention of the drink, nor the news for which he had been longing.

Susie arrived with her scarf. They said their goodbyes, Jane thanked him, and the door closed immediately.

They hurried towards the Fisherman's Arms. For the child's sake, she made an effort at normal conversation.

"I hope you didn't have too much to eat with Mr. Pate, and spoil your supper. "What *did* you have?"

"Nothing."

"No marzipan mouse?"

"I just watched television."

"No banana splits? No ice-creams?"

"There were people talking."

"Where did you watch TV?"

"In a little room. He asked me all about you, then he closed the door. There was a lady."

"I thought I saw one. What did she look like?"

"I didn't see. She spoke funny."

Could it have been Stephanie Hirsch? Could the flash of red have been her cerise mohair skirt? But Pate had not recognised her description of the woman in the pharmacy. Or pretended not to. Elegant. Foreign accent. He must have known whom she meant. She felt a growing unease.

"Did you hear anything they said?"

"No." Susie had lost interest and was scraping her shoes across the sidewalk.

"Don't do that. You'll wear them out. Wasn't there another man with Mr. Pate, too?"

"He came in afterwards. Miss Blackstock knew him. She doesn't like him."

Jane's heart lurched. "And who does Miss Blackstock think he is?"

"The shouty man."

"What shouty man?"

"He shouted at me. He's got a beard."

"Mr. da Souza?"

"They were talking loudly."

"What about?"

But Susie stared at her blankly and began to drag at her hand. "Miss Blackstock's hungry," she said, and Jane knew she would get nothing more out of her about Pate's visitors.

Because it had been a sunny day, carloads of sightseers had driven out to Margate from Boston and some had stayed on for an evening meal. The restaurant at the Fisherman's Arms was busy. There was no sign of David. A young waitress was helping Peter, who had no time for conversation. And Jane had little appetite. The memory of the battered body in the surf and the silent figure in the ruined house was haunting her.

When they returned to the cottage, Jane settled Susie in her bed. She felt tired, but it was not the healthy physical tiredness she might have expected after a day on the beach. Her mind was filled with conflicting emotions. It was as though she had, almost overnight, become enmeshed in a series of events which she did not understand and over which she had little control. Her peaceful haven had become a place of mysteries. Pictures formed in her inner eye, images which were there one moment and gone the next: Pate's plump hands concocting a banana split, his eyes cold in the pink, baby face; Stephanie Hirsch talking with apparent intimacy to David; the awful battered head of the log that had not been a log; Chief Boyd; the lonely house with sand on its broken floors; David, kissing her. That had been the high spot of the day—the high spot of a great many days. She could not even recall how long it had been since a man had kissed her.

There was a knock at the beach door.

"It's me." David's voice.

He had a bottle in his hand. "I've brought some brandy. I thought you might need it."

As she fetched glasses she thought that in that long,

disturbing day he had seemed to be the one stable element. Yet even he was not entirely straightforward. He had not attempted to explain why he had not turned up the previous night. He had offered an apology, but no excuses. After her questions about the Swiss woman, he had not mentioned her again. Was he the kind of man who liked running two women at once? Had he come here now, directly from her? Questions, questions, she thought wearily. And no answers.

David warmed the brandy-glass between his hands before sipping it. "How's Susie?"

"Fine. She's asleep." She closed the bedroom door. "We needn't whisper. I don't think she understood what happened this afternoon. She didn't see the body."

"You talked to Chief Boyd?"

"He took a statement. I have to sign it tomorrow."

"He took one from me as well."

"Did you find anything else on the beach?"

"No. We searched the full length and in the dunes until it got dark."

They talked about the day and, even as they speculated about the dead man's identity, its horrors began to recede.

"Bodies do get washed ashore occasionally, especially from the shipping lanes," he said. "People get washed overboard, or jump over. The Boston police are always fishing corpses out of the Charles River."

"Chief Boyd seems to take its arrival as a personal affront."

"He's short-staffed in winter. They only expect things like this to happen in summer."

There was a brief silence, then she said: "David, I *did* see a man in that house."

His voice was tired. "I believe you. I heard the car, too. But he couldn't have had anything to do with the body, Jane. That poor guy had been dead for a couple of days, I'd guess. It was probably someone sheltering from the storm, as you were."

"Then why didn't he speak to us. Why did he hide in the closet and then just stand there, watching?"

112

"Maybe he got as big a fright as you did. Maybe he was shy."

"That's silly. If you hadn't come . . . "

"He'd probably have greeted you like any normal man running into a pretty girl in a deserted house, and talked about the weather. I scared him off. Did you tell Boyd about him?"

"Yes. I had the impression he thought I'd imagined the whole thing."

"Don't make any mistake about Chief Boyd. He's as shrewd as they come. You can be sure he'll look into it."

"Someone must have seen the car."

"If so, Boyd will find out. Incidentally, we found where it had been parked. There were tyre-marks and oil in the sand just off the road, a few hundred yards from the parking-lot. They were behind a dune."

"So he'd deliberately hidden it."

"Not necessarily. There's no particular reason why anyone should use the lot out of season. Don't let this get to you, I don't think there was any sinister motive in his choice of a parking-place."

Don't let this get to you. She was suddenly reminded of Walter and the man he had hired to persecute her in London. But Walter was far away and this could have nothing to do with him. David refilled her glass and said: "Until the end, it was a good day. I'd hate to think you'll only remember the bad bits."

"I won't," she said. "The good bits were—special."

After her second brandy she was feeling slightly more cheerful, but she shook her head when he brought the bottle over to her.

"I'll have a hang-over in the morning."

"Not with this. It's five-star."

She accepted a small one. Then she said, idly, "I think I saw your lady friend again."

"Lady friend? Which one?"

"The elegant Madame Hirsch. She was at Dennis Pate's house. Or I'm pretty sure she was."

113

"How do you know?" His voice was sharp.

"I left Susie with Pate when I went to see Chief Boyd. She was there."

"Did you actually see her?"

She disappeared as he opened the door. She obviously didn't want to be seen. She was still there when I picked Susie up, talking to Pate and da Souza."

He drained his brandy and yawned elaborately. "No reason I know of they shouldn't be friends. Wow, I'm bushed! Nothing like a day in the open to make you sleepy, especially when it includes finding a dead body."

She looked at her watch and said: "Margate certainly retires early."

"We need our sleep. Anyway, you should talk. You must have been out cold when I dropped that note in about eleven last night. I knocked. Place was in darkness, not a sound."

He let himself out of the door to the beach and she locked it behind him. The room was suddenly empty. This was a very odd relationship they had built up, she thought. It was on two distinct levels: the surface one, based on what they said and did; the hidden one of tensions and thoughts and suspicions and mysteries, where nothing was as it seemed. Like Susie's blue and red men . . .

He had left the brandy bottle, but she did not feel like another drink. She did not feel like going to bed, either. When she went to sleep early she tended to wake in the dead hours between two and four. Like last night.

Something suddenly came back to her. David said he had dropped the note in around eleven. But it had been two o'clock when she had woken up and heard the scuffling and bumping and someone trying her door. If that had not been David, who had it been?

Her fears returned, primitive fears of the dark. She left her light on and read until her eyes were sore, but she took a long time to sleep. And all the time she was listening for scuffling, scraping noises at the door.

8

Once again the weather had changed. It reminded her of England, for when she opened the door to the beach she found that very cold air had moved in and great masses of cloud were passing overhead. Again she felt the tug of homesickness.

She prepared breakfast for Susie and, as they were still sitting at the table, David arrived, clearly in sombre mood. "Can we talk?" he said.

Producing the much-used means to a few moments' privacy, she said to Susie: "You want to watch television?"

"I want to go to the beach."

Jane hesitated.

"She'll be all right," David said. "There's no one about."

"As long as you play in front of the cottage."

They watched her leave the sun-deck and resume her interminable search for shells and pebbles.

"I saw Chief Boyd half an hour ago," he said.

"You were up early."

"They've identified the body. He was a New York PI."

"What's that?"

"Private investigator. Private detective."

"I wonder what . . . oh, my God! David, he could have been . . . "

"Looking for you. I know. There's something I didn't want to tell you yesterday, but now it makes sense: I think he was the man who came to the hotel looking for a room late the other night."

She took a deep breath and closed her eyes for a second. "When I arrived here I thought I'd found a sort of heaven.

No one knew me.'' She paused. ''You don't *know* he was looking for Susie and me. That's only a guess, isn't it?'' Her voice had risen.

''Sure. But look at it logically. It fits.''

''Here we go again, always logical and rational. Sorry, I didn't mean that. Go ahead.''

''Your ex-husband . . . ''

''Ex-husband sounds like something out of a court case.''

''Hemming says he'll look for you, he'll find you. What he means is, he'll hire someone to do it. There's only one group of citizens he could go to. Private investigators.''

''So that man in the blue parka . . . ''

''That's it, if my hunch is right. Hemming took him to the court to see you, so he'd recognise you and Susie again. And he followed you to your New York hotel and made some inquiries and found you'd gone to Boston.''

''But I didn't tell anyone where I was going.''

''No one at all? Think.''

''I didn't even book seats. Just went to Penn Station, bought tickets and got on to the train.'' She stopped. ''Oh, Lord! Tony.''

''Tony?''

''A reservations clerk at the hotel. He wanted to take us to dinner. I was so surprised I said, without thinking, that we were leaving for Boston.''

''A reservations clerk in your hotel would be one of the first people a PI would approach. More inquiries, about half a day, to find where you stayed in Boston. A few questions. A few dollars to the bell captain . . . ''

''He recommended a travel agency where I could book our airline seats to London. A clerk there told me about the Fisherman's Arms.''

''You couldn't have made it easier for him if you'd drawn a map. So he followed you here, arrived late and came straight to the hotel.''

''And when you wouldn't let him have a room?''

116

"Probably went back to a motel in Chatham or Hyannis."

"And came here during the day to check on us. Maybe he was waiting for Walter—and the chance to grab Susie." She thought of the scuffling at her door. The detective? Or Walter himself?

"It looks like it."

"Could he have been the man Susie saw on the dunes?"

"It's possible. But remember we don't even know for sure if there was a man there, or if it was human blood I found."

"But it could have been. And Susie said she saw something red. It might have been blood around his wound."

She went to the window. The small figure had drifted down towards the jetty where the big truck still stood. Jane shouted and beckoned for her to come back. As she watched Susie, she said: "That would mean someone murdered him."

"We don't *know* if it was the same man, and there could be some other explanation. We don't have any facts."

"Facts!" She began pacing up and down the room. "Life isn't made up of facts! It's made up of fragments, shadows, half-remembered thoughts, assumptions, guesses, intuitions. I think you believe he came here to look for me. I agree with you. And I think he was murdered just before Susie found him. I think that whoever killed him saw Susie and hid until she had come rushing back to me. Then they took him out to sea and dumped him, or threw him from a cliff. But why? What's going on in this place?"

"Jane . . ." She waited for him to continue, but he seemed to catch himself, as though he had changed his mind about whatever he had been going to say. "It's only speculation. And you'd better keep it to yourself, especially around Boyd. If he were to find out about you and Hemming, you might be held as a material witness."

"You mean they'd hold me here?" The thought frightened her more than anything so far. "What would happen to Susie?"

"There's nothing to connect you with the dead man so far.

117

Look, I'll call you later. But stay close." He took her hand and put it to his lips. "I don't want anything happening to you."

Soon after he had left, a policeman named Ellis arrived at her door and told her the Chief was ready to have her sign her statement.

"So this is your kid," Boyd said, motioning them to chairs. "Lucky she was asleep. This here's what you said yesterday. What I want is that you read it through and make sure it's correct, then sign it. You understand?"

She looked into the hard square face, the pale-fringed eyes and, for the first time in her life, felt fear of a policeman.

She read the typed sheets quickly. It was a spare, professional statement; it left nothing out and added nothing. As she checked it, Boyd stared at her.

"That's fine," she said.

He passed her a pen and she signed, then he turned to Susie and said, "You having a nice vacation?"

"We go for walks on the sands."

"That's nice." He was making a visible effort at grace.

"The man was asleep."

"That's right. The man was asleep. A long, long sleep."

"Miss Blackstock knows him."

"Who?"

"Susie . . ." Jane said warningly.

"On the beach. The blue man. Miss Blackstock . . ."

"Who's Miss Blackstock?" Boyd said.

"Her scarf," Jane said.

"Her *what*?"

She pointed to the scarf. "It can be any imaginary person Susie likes. Often she calls it Miss Blackstock."

"Uh-huh," he said, losing interest.

"The blue man was asleep on the sand. And red . . ." She was about to show where the red had been when the telephone rang.

Boyd picked it up. "Yeah?" He reached for his pen and began making notes. "Two 1s? A *what*? Yeah. Got it. You

118

sure? Yeah, well, that's what it looked like, only I wasn't sure. Okay, we'll take it from here."

He put the phone down and sighed. "That was Boston. They got an ID on the . . ." He glanced at the child. "On the man."

"The blue man," Susie said. "Miss Blackstock said . . ."

"Name of Willis. Harry Willis. A private investigator from New York."

Jane felt a prickling sensation at the back of her neck. "Do they know what happened?"

"They know he didn't drown. No water in the lungs. They think it might have been the back of an axe or an iron bar. Something like that."

She moistened her lips. "Do they know why he was here?"

"That's not their job; that's mine. We'll check it in New York first. Maybe he had a partner. Maybe he had a secretary. Maybe he kept files."

"Do you think he did?"

"What?"

"Keep files."

"Mrs. Hemming, I've been in police work seventeen years and if there's one thing I've learnt it's don't speculate. I know some PIs who have got offices like . . . well, better than mine. Green metal cabinets full of information. Some have even got computers. I know others who've got nothing. Everything's up here." He tapped his forehead. "Maybe we'll get lucky. Maybe not. How long are you going to be staying?"

"Another four days."

"If I need you for anything, I can get you at the hotel, right?"

"Yes."

There was a knock at the door. Ellis came in, carrying a large plastic bag. "This was washed up on Shoal Point," he said. "Some time in the night, I guess."

"What is it?"

He opened the mouth of the bag. "Blue parka."

Susie opened her mouth but Jane, who had frozen

119

momentarily, reached for her hand. "Not now, darling," she whispered.

"Anything in the pockets?" Boyd said.

"Haven't looked yet." He pulled out a bundle of greyish, matted wool. He shook it, and as it elongated, Jane saw again the evil clown's face, the red-rimmed eyes and mouth that had leered at her from the Buick as she had been on her way to Plymouth.

"It's a ski-mask," Boyd said. "What's a PI doing with a ski-mask? See if there's anything else, Chuck."

Ellis explored the other pocket. "Nothing . . . oh, yes." He held up a small, hairy object.

"What the hell's that?" Boyd said.

"It's sort of attached—hey, it's a false moustache, for Christ's sake!"

Jane was thankful they were too absorbed in their finds to be aware of her stifled gasp.

Then Susie, tugging at her skirt, said excitedly: "The blue man! The blue man and the red man!"

A look of interest appeared on Boyd's face as he turned to her, the moustache still in his hand. "Does she mean this blue parka?"

"Miss Blackstock knows the blue man . . . "

"No!" Jane said. "It's just a story she's been telling Miss Blackstock. She saw lots of men wearing blue parkas in New York."

He bent towards Susie. "What's the story about?"

Was he suspicious, or was it a polite gesture to a child? Jane said hastily, "It's just about a blue man and a red man and how they chase a girl."

Susie was jumping up and down, chanting: "The blue man. The blue man."

"And the scarf's Miss Blackstock, huh?"

"Or sometimes Sir Henry. Or the Prince," Jane said, covering the subject in confusion. The look of interest faded from Boyd's face. He shook his head. "I guess I never did understand small children."

"Is that all you want us for?"

"That's all for now. We haven't been able to trace that guy you claim you saw in the house, by the way. We're still trying."

"Come on, Susie."

"But Mummy, Miss Blackstock . . ."

She hauled the child out into the street, desperate to get home, to be by herself and try to make sense of what she had just seen.

"Never mind Miss Blackstock! Let's see if we can buy something nice for lunch." She could feel Susie's chagrin transmitted through her fingers. She didn't want to make an issue of the blue man, exaggerating his importance, but she realised that she would have to be constantly on guard against the child's artless confidences in public. Fortunately, Boyd had simply been puzzled by her oblique view of the world. Jane wanted his confusion to remain.

But once she reached the cottage, with time to review what had happened, she realised that she was in a state of even greater confusion.

Her discovery that Harry Willis, the dead man, and the man who had lured Susie from the hotel room in Boston, and the driver in the ski-mask were one and the same, was almost too much for her to absorb. Yet she had no doubt that it was so.

Why would he have adopted his comic-strip disguises? Why the charade in the hotel? Why would he have pursued her in his car, then disappeared?

Slowly, the inescapable answer to all the questions came: Walter had been one step ahead of her. He had hired Willis to watch her. She had given him the slip in New York but, as David had suggested, it had been a simple matter for him to trace her. He had flown up on the shuttle and been waiting for her in Boston, planning to kidnap Susie. It was sheer good luck that he had not been able to carry out his plan, and that the police's speedtrap had scared him off at his second attempt.

But now he was dead, brutally murdered, and for that she had no explanation. Nor for the identity of the man in the house on the dunes. Perhaps David's dismissal of him as a significant element had been correct.

David himself was the centre of another mystery and there was one major question for which she could find no answer: *How could he have known, so early this morning, who the dead man was?*

He had said he had seen Chief Boyd. Yet she had been in Boyd's office nearly an hour later when he had taken the call identifying the body. He had been told the man's name was Harry Willis. He had not known it earlier, because she had heard him ask if it was spelt with two Ls. David had not mentioned the name, but had known that the man was a private investigator. Boyd had not known that, either.

As she cast her mind back over the past few days she saw herself in a kind of Kafka-esque world in which nothing was as it seemed: a nightmare in which everyone wore a mask, and when you pulled off one, you found another underneath. Pate and Fischer claimed to be writer and artist respectively, but she had seen no evidence of work from either. And what of Stephanie Hirsch, whose acquaintance nobody wanted to admit, but whose presence was so pervasive? And David, always David, the one she knew best, and at the same time, least. The one to whom she had come closest, the most elusive. She thought of his abrupt changes of mood, his brusqueness, his sudden disappearances and reappearances. She thought of his humour and his intelligence, his logic, his strength. And yet, the questions remained: how had he known the body's identity? And why had he come to tell her about it before she went to see Chief Boyd? He must have known there was a risk she might realise Boyd had not given him the information. He had been prepared to take the risk. She recalled him advising her to keep silent, not to involve herself lest she be caught up in the affair as a material witness. Had he been trying to frighten her into silence.

One thing was sure: at the moment, she could not leave,

for Boyd had made it plain he wanted to keep tabs on her. She wondered briefly whether she might not simply pack the car and make a run for it. Drive to New York, get herself and Susie on to the first plane to anywhere, Canada, South America, perhaps, then fly home from there. But they could easily be stopped. Some agent of Boyd's might even now be going through a filing cabinet in Harry Willis's office and uncovering the contract between Willis and a man named Walter Hemming. All it would take would be the name. She thought of the effect on Susie of the endless questions, the publicity, Walter's arrival to remove his daughter.

The beach cottage had seemed like a sanctuary but now, with an implied restriction on her movements, it was becoming a kind of prison and she found herself looking at it with new eyes, disliking it. What she had first thought of as simple holiday charm she now saw as cheap bad taste. The small rooms were cramped and claustrophobic. The mood of that first day, when she had awakened in the sunshine, was gone. It had become a setting of fear and confusion, of inquiries that destroyed her privacy.

Susie was hunched in the bedroom watching television, a corner of the scarf in her mouth.

"Come on, darling," Jane called. "Let's get out of here for a while."

"It's cold."

"We'll wrap up."

She did not want to take the road to the beach, for both it and the dunes were now filled with terrors. Instead, they walked through the town and began to climb the hill. Soon they left the houses behind and came out on to a promontory covered in grass and low bush that overlooked the harbour. It was very cold and her eyes began to water. Then she saw the bearded figure of Peter Davidson sitting at his easel some yards to her left.

He looked up. "Hi!" he said. He was dressed in a heavy beige parka and a knitted hat, but his hands were bare and purple with cold.

"You must be freezing."

"I've been out in worse."

She came behind him and looked at the painting. It was unlike his other work. Instead of the semi-abstract seascapes and dunescapes which had attracted her in the hotel lobby, this one was conventional to the point of cliché. He was painting exactly what he saw: the roofs of the houses below, the harbour, the jetty, the fishing-smacks, the big truck, all expressed in obvious colours an amateur might have chosen. She was reminded of village art-society exhibitions in England.

"What do you think of it?"

"It's . . . interesting."

"No, it's not. It's terrible. But it's the sort of thing your blue-rinsed lady from Dubuque will buy when she's here on vacation in July."

"What about your others?"

"No sale. That's why they're hanging in the hotel."

"Have you tried them on the visitors?"

"Sure. Come summer, I put them in the restaurant with prices on them. Maybe I've been asking too much, but whatever the reason, they haven't made it."

"Isn't this, sort of, cheating?"

"Maybe. But you see that?" He pointed to an ageing yellow Chrysler which was parked a hundred yards away. "That's about all I've got. That and my dune-buggy and an ex-wife and two kids and alimony payments every month. If the tourists want junk, I'll give them junk. I've done a dozen or more scenes round the harbour. Quaint. I reckon I can sell them out of the restaurant at two hundred bucks apiece in the summer. By that time I'll have twenty or thirty more. And then . . ."

"Then ?"

"Then I'll take off. Spain. France. Italy. And I'll paint as I want to."

"Money doesn't last long in Europe."

"I'll make it."

124

She smiled at his enthusiasm and forbore to remind him that even garrets in Paris were now chic and expensive, as they were in the South of France, Spain and Italy; that he was living in a dream that had faded years before.

"You can't live in a garret forever," she said.

"I don't aim to."

"And when you come back?"

"I'll buy the Fisherman's Arms and it'll be *mine* and I'll have someone working for *me*. And when I want to paint, I'll paint and when I don't, I won't."

"That takes real money."

"I plan to have real money."

"Not from painting scenes of the harbour."

"No, not painting scenes of the harbour." He rubbed his hands and stood up. "It's too cold to do any more. Let me have a minute to pack up and I'll give you a ride back." She watched him put away his brushes and paints in an old wooden box. From the ground beside him he picked up a pair of powerful Zeiss binoculars which looked like the ones David used for bird-watching—if it was bird-watching—and, without comment, slung them around his neck.

9

She had hardly closed the cottage door when the telephone rang. It was David. Instead of the usual lift she felt on hearing his voice, she was wary.

"Have you seen Boyd?" he said.

"Yes."

"And?"

"I signed my statement."

He waited. "Is that all?"

"No."

"You sound as though there was trouble."

She did not reply.

"Was there? Something important?"

"It was to me."

"Want to tell me?"

She thought for a moment. Shouldn't she at least give him an opportunity to explain the time discrepancy between his identification of the body and Boyd's? If he was keeping something from her, it would be more difficult for him to continue the deception face to face. Finally she said, "Yes, but not on the phone."

"How about getting away from here for a while? Lunch. The three of us. You can tell me about it then."

"All right. But no more picnics."

"We couldn't anyway, in this cold. I know a restaurant down the coast that is supposed to have the best seafood on the Cape. It's not the Ritz, but I'm told it's the place if you like broiled lobster or fried clams."

After he picked her up they drove out along Route Six, then took the road along the inner Cape. Susie was tucked under a blanket in the back of the car. She was in a chatty mood, making it difficult for Jane and David to talk freely. At first Jane was aware of his questioning glances, but he had apparently decided to await a moment when Susie's attention could be diverted before bringing up the subject that was on both their minds. He said nothing untoward, and she was grateful for his restraint, not wanting the child to hear anything which might make her curious about yesterday's events. As they headed towards the sea on minor roads, the country changed. There were pines bordering the road and beyond them she could see marshland.

"Cranberry bogs," he said, pointing to man-made depressions like huge baking trays to their left. Each covered ten or more acres and the cranberry vines grew like close ground-cover, russet in the cold light.

They pulled up outside a weathered, clapboard building covered in faded Coca Cola signs. It was called "Uncle's". Some of the boards had worked loose in the winter winds and it had a seedy air. It stood by itself just off the road and she could not see another building anywhere at hand. The area was sandy, with occasional pine trees and the acres of cranberry bogs.

They parked and walked towards the restaurant. Susie ran ahead and then veered away to the left, down a slope. "Look! Berries!" she cried.

"Hey!" David caught her at the edge of the bog. "You don't want to go in there, honey."

There were still some red cranberries left from the recently-harvested crop and they looked inviting. But then Jane saw that the bog was inches deep in water, being filled from a pipe some distance away.

"It's not deep enough yet to drown her, but in a few hours you'll be able to skate on those bogs," he said. "In really cold weather they flood them and let ice form. It protects the plants from frost and freezing winds."

They each took one of Susie's hands and went up the bank towards the restaurant. The inside of Uncle's was more promising than the exterior. There were wooden booths around the walls, with a horse-shoe bar in the middle. Several booths were occupied and two men crouched on stools at the bar.

They stood for a moment, allowing their eyes to become adjusted to the dimness, then took their seats in a booth. "I wonder why you keep your bars so dark?" Jane said idly.

"We're still Puritans at heart. Basically, we think boozing is shameful, so we do it in half darkness. That having been said, what's yours?"

They ordered martinis and looked at the menu. "What's piri-piri?" she asked.

"Portuguese hot sauce."

"I'd like the lobster piri-piri."

They ordered and sat back, sipping their drinks. Then Susie saw a Space Invaders game at the far side of the room and went over to play it. At once, David said: "You said there was trouble. What's happened?"

Jane hesitated as she grouped her thoughts, then said carefully: "You told me that man was a private investigator from New York."

"Right."

"That was early this morning. When I was with Chief Boyd later he took a call from Boston. He was only told then who the man was."

"So?"

"You said you'd been told the identity of the body by Boyd."

"Whoa!" he said, holding up his hand. "I didn't say that. I said I'd seen Boyd. That was to sign the statement. You must have assumed he'd told me about the body."

"If he didn't, who did? I mean, how did *you* know before the local chief of police?"

His eyes were guileless. "If that's all that's worrying you, I can set your imagination at rest. I have a friend in the Boston police department. We were at law school together. I called him. He told me what they'd discovered."

"Why did you call him?"

"Because of you." He placed one of his hands on hers. "Look, Jane, you've had enough problems. I wanted to find out who he was so I could prepare you before you saw Boyd. So you wouldn't blurt out something that might hurt you."

She felt a flood of relief. "Oh, God, I've been so worried! I thought—I don't know what I thought . . . "

"Was that the only thing worrying you?"

"Far from it!" She told him about her discovery of the dead man's triple identity, her certainty now that somewhere in the background of the whole situation, Walter lurked. For once he had no comfort to offer, no rational explanation as an alternative to her own.

"I think the only thing we can do now is play it by ear." he said slowly. "The guy's dead. If you're right, the next move will be up to your ex-husband. Jane, I want you and Susie to transfer into the hotel, where I can keep an eye on you."

"It's closed, remember?"

"I'm learning to be flexible," he said grimly.

"All right. When?"

"Soon as you can . . . " He stopped as their food arrived at the table. Susie returned simultaneously.

Feeling that they could not take the conversation further for the moment, they reverted to trivialities. The lobster was hot and spicy and Jane ate it with good appetite.

Half way through the meal Susie whispered to her.

"Now?" Jane said.

"Yes. Now."

On their way back from the ladies' room they heard a voice. "Princess!"

The two men at the bar had turned towards them. One was the fisherman from Margate. Frank da Souza. The other was younger, with shining hair swept back and long black side-burns.

"How's the Princess?" da Souza said loudly. Then, to his friend: "This is a real English princess. You gotta hear her talk!" He turned to Jane. "Come on, let me buy you both a drink."

"No, thanks, we're . . ."

"You a princess, too?" the other man said. He was about twenty, thickset and powerful. He was wearing a white T-shirt which showed off his chest to some effect.

She ignored him and said to da Souza, "No, really . . ."

"No, re-ahlly . . ." the younger man said, his face impassive.

"You trying to speak English? A wop like you?" da Souza said, grinning. "You tell him, Princess. Julio ain't never going to speak good English."

"Maybe she could teach me," Julio said, still looking at Jane. She had the impression of something feral peering out from behind the small, dark eyes. "No, really . . . Is that how you speak English? I say, old chap . . . how splendid . . . Is that English?"

She said: "We're in the middle of lunch. I must go back."

"I *want* to learn," Julio said, and she realised they must have been drinking for some time. "I catch these guys on TV. I say, old chap . . . pip-pip. That can't be right. I mean, those guys in London, with the bowler hats, do they go round saying pip-pip? I want to learn it right. Maybe you can teach me. There are things I can teach you, too."

She reached for Susie's hand. He moved closer, touching her. "There's no hurry. Frank says, have a drink. Why not be a little friendly?"

"Hello, Frank." David was standing beside them.

Da Souza peered through the gloom. "Oh, hi, Dave."

"Hi, Dave," Julio said, his face blank again.

David ignored him. "Your lunch is getting cold," he said.

Jane nodded to the men and turned away, but Julio gripped her arm. "When you going to teach me English?" he said softly.

David swung around, frowning ominously, but she put a restraining hand on his arm. "I only teach people who know how to behave," she said coldly.

Julio's head jerked as though she had slapped him and she was aware of his eyes following her as they returned to the booth.''

"That drunken lout should be thrown out!" David said. "Sorry about that, Jane."

She shrugged. "It's all right. I'm glad there wasn't a scene."

"You'll never know how close you were to one," he said grimly.

They finished their meal in silence. She noticed that David kept glancing towards the men and hoped that there would be no further trouble. He made hardly any pretence at small talk. When da Souza and Julio stood up to leave, he called for the bill. The waitress was slow and when they reached the car park a battered truck, driven by da Souza was already turning on to the road. David reached the car ten paces ahead of her and had already started the engine by the time she put Susie into the back seat. She had only time to scramble into the front and had not even closed the door when he took off. She was about to speak when he said abruptly, "I thought we'd go for a drive. The country round here is worth seeing." He turned in the direction da Souza had taken, but the truck was out of sight and within half a mile the road split. David said nothing, but she saw his lips form a thin, irritated line and she realised that for some reason he had wanted to follow da Souza. She was relieved that the van had disappeared.

After a brief hesitation he took the left fork and they drove past more cranberry bogs. The silence continued. As much to break it as from a wish to talk, she said, "I enjoyed my lunch. Did you?"

He did not reply, apparently preoccupied with the road and the countryside. She shrugged and settled into her corner. They came on through the bogs and sea-marshes near Sandwich and then along a road by the beach.

Suddenly Susie said: "The thin man's car."

Jane glanced around and saw she was pointing to a brown car parked on a deserted stretch of road they had just passed.

131

Beyond it was a line of wooden cottages and, beyond them, the beach.

"What does she mean?" David said.

"She thinks that car belongs to Dennis Pate's German friend."

Taking her by surprise, he braked, made a U-turn and drove slowly back along the road until they reached the brown car. "Are you sure it's Fischer's?" he said.

"Susie remembers cars. And we nearly had an accident because of him the other day."

"We must be getting back," he said abruptly, and swung towards the Mid-Cape Highway, driving faster than usual.

When they reached Margate, he dropped them in the middle of the town, with a brief apology and a muttered remark about hotel business.

"Will I see you later?" she said. "When should we bring our things over to the hotel?"

"I'll call you."

Once again she felt let down. At one moment, the look in his eyes, the touch of his hand, told her that he was attracted to her. The next, he was abstracted and indifferent, treating her with no more warmth than a passing acquaintance. She found it difficult to stay with his moods. She tried to tell herself that there was no reason for her to mind, but she did. In spite of her suspicions about his relationship with Stephanie Hirsch, in spite of his unpredictability, she felt herself increasingly drawn to him. Perhaps it was partly because he was the only person in Margate who knew her story and had shown sympathy and support; but part, she knew, was something else, and that something else hardly bore analysis in her present situation.

She watched the car disappear. Dusk was falling and it was freezing hard. She and Susie hurried through the empty streets.

She almost knocked Dennis Pate down before she noticed him. "Good afternoon, my dear!" he said. "This is well met. I was coming to see our princess." He smiled down at Susie.

"What would you say if I carried her off and we created another of those magnificent confections." Susie looked at him blankly. "I mean another banana split." Her face lit up.

Why not? Jane thought. The child would enjoy it and she herself would welcome the chance to be alone for an hour or so.

"Would you like that, darling?"

"Yes, please."

"Come along, then," Pate said. "Let's go and see what we can find."

He held out a heavily-gloved hand. Susie wound her scarf, which had alternated between the Prince and Miss Blackstock all day, around her neck, and put her tiny, mittened hand into his. Jane watched them go up the road, like Pooh and Piglet off on an adventure.

She walked onto the beach just past the hotel. It was deserted. Even the truck had gone from the jetty. She ploughed through the sand, climbed the steps onto the sun-deck and let herself into the cottage. As she closed the door, a man cleared his throat in the semi-darkness behind her.

She gasped, and switched on the light. Walter was sitting in the armchair. It seemed as though all her motor functions had collapsed. Her heart stopped beating and she ceased, for a moment, to breathe.

"Hello, Jane."

"How did you get in?"

He gestured towards the warped street door. "You forgot to lock it."

She had kept as far away from him as possible in court and had forgotten how large he was. He wore a heavy, dark grey herring-bone overcoat and a claret-coloured scarf. The chair looked too small to hold him. She saw the big, soft hands and the gold signet ring she had given him, and the circular scar on the left side of his face from a childhood attack of shingles. The pores on his face were like tiny craters. She had noticed in New York how he now combed his dark hair sideways to hide an increasing bald patch. He was fatter, too.

133

His cheeks were plump and jowly and his muddy eyes were cold.

She tried to speak, but no sound emerged. Her larynx felt paralysed.

"I told you I'd find you," he said softly.

"What do you want?"

"What I've always wanted."

She shook her head. "You're not getting Susie."

He leaned back in the chair. There was something knowing about him, an arrogant confidence that had always made her uneasy; it was as though he knew he was one mental jump ahead of her.

"Are we going to be civilised?" he said.

"It depends on what you mean by civilised."

"For a start, how about offering me a cup of coffee?"

She was about to say that he would not be around long enough to drink it, then thought that would sound childish. She had time. Pate would not be returning Susie for an hour or so.

She made him a cup of instant coffee. He had been accustomed to take cream and sugar, now he held up his hand when she offered them. "Straight." He smiled, with the same cold eyes. "Remember how you used to watch your weight? Me too, now. Aren't you having one?"

"I don't want any."

He sipped his drink and stared at her through the steam. She felt he was stripping her with his eyes. "You look good."

"Thank you."

"I remember the first time I saw you in London. I thought what a terrific looker you were. You're better now. You were too thin then. I like my women . . ." He held out his hands and formed a shape in the air. "Ripe."

She thought of the early days when those hands had crawled over her. A vision of his naked body came to her. The irony was that he was going bald, yet there was a mat of black hair all over his chest and belly and a kind of thin fur on his shoulder-blades. She had told herself at first that she did not mind it, but she had.

"Where's Susie?" he said.

"Why?"

"You know why."

The civilised veneer dropped away as though it had never been; now it was two savage dogs called Walter and Jane fighting again over this bone called Susie.

"She's not here."

"That's obvious. That's why I asked." He kept his voice low, but she could see his fingers laced together, tight with tension. He picked up his cup again, drained it and set it back in its saucer. "Did you really think I would let you keep my daughter?"

"You have no choice. You heard what the judge said."

"Let me tell you something: I don't give a fuck what any judge says. No one's going to tell me I can't have my own child. She's mine. She has my blood, my genes. No one's going to get in my way. Not you. Nobody."

"Are you threatening me?"

"You're damn right."

"What do you think would happen if I called the police?"

"Sweetie, you're in *my* country. You want to play games with me, go ahead. Try it."

"I'd take you to court again."

He laughed. "Where? I'm moving up in the world. My travelling days are over. UPH have put me in overall control of their South American enterprises, headquarters in Rio. That's where Susie and I'll be living. The Brazilian courts have no jurisdiction, baby."

She felt her stomach knot.

He went on: "Have you seen this?" He pulled a copy of the *Cape Cod Times* from his coat pocket, put it on the table in front of her and tapped a double-column story on page one. "Read it."

The heading said: NEW YORK PI DROWNS ON CAPE BEACH: She read the story with growing dread. There were

135

no new facts, but now she was seeing them through Walter's eyes. It was what David had warned her might happen.

"You want to tell me he was drowned while he was swimming? Fully-dressed?" Walter said.

"I don't know anything about him."

"Come on, sweetie! He'd traced you. He was reporting to me. I know the facts. You saw him in New York. You knew him when he came here."

"You sent him to kidnap Susie."

"In Boston?" He laughed. "He told me about that. And about the ski-mask. That really got to you, didn't it?" His voice was vindictive. "He was giving you a taste of what you'll be suffering if you try to keep her away from me. I'll never give you any peace, Jane. I'll get her in the end, one way or another, and in the meantime, you'll never know what I'm going to try next. Willis is dead. You found some way to get rid of him. But there'll be other Willises."

"No!"

"Let me tell you something. You pick up that phone and talk to the cops and I'm going to start talking, too. What do you think they're going to say when I tell them that I hired a New York detective to track down my wife and daughter? In terms of the court judgement, maybe I was doing wrong. But a father loves his daughter, even cops can understand that. I only wanted to see her, what's wrong with that? Anyway, the detective finds you and as soon as he does, he's kaput. Now do you want to think again about calling the police? Let me ask you this once more: where's Susie?"

A dozen lies came into her head. She wanted to say: "She's on a plane to England. She's back with her grandmother, out of your reach." What was the point? He had found them, just as he had said he would. And she knew he was right about the police. This was his country and so far he had not broken any laws. All he had done was hire a private investigator, who had found his daughter, and who was now dead.

She saw a black pit yawning before her, with sides so smooth that if she fell in, she would never be able to climb out. She saw herself, Jane Hemming, as the accused in a murder trial. She saw her daughter taken away for ever by the father to whom she was no more than another possession.

Her steady gaze, fixed on Walter, gave no hint of her thoughts. Instinct told her to waste time, to keep him talking until she could figure a way to escape him. But time was what she did not have. All too soon, there would be a knock at the door and Dennis Pate would be returning Susie.

Walter had backed her into a corner. What if she were to tell Boyd the whole story? Whose side would he take? Walter was Mr. Fixit. He knew how to play on people's greed; he had spent years in charge of a slush fund. Was Chief Boyd incorruptible? She could not take the chance. There must be another way. David. Where was he? How could she reach him? Anyway he, too, was an uknown quantity. She could rely on no one but herself.

The street door was not locked, and she was not more than two yards from it. Walter was still in his chair, between her and the sun-deck door. His long, thick legs were stretched out, his eyes half-closed, watching her, waiting for her to give in.

Her reactions had always been fast. Now, with the adrenalin rushing through her muscles, she launched herself at the door. She took him by surprise and was there before he reacted. He pushed himself up from the chair and lumbered after her. She reached for the door-handle and pulled. Had it opened smoothly, she might have had a chance. But it stuck. She felt his hands grab her.

She knew what would happen next. It had happened before. During their marriage she had always been afraid to fight back, afraid that if she did, she would anger him still further and that he would disfigure her. But now, with Susie's future in the balance, fear was dispelled by panic and panic by rage. He was not going to have Susie. Not now. Not ever. She twisted, and managed to get one hand free. The nails were long and sharp and she brought them down his face, feeling the skin collect under them like wax.

"Christ!" he said.

He felt his cheek and his hand came away with blood on it. He looked at it in disbelief. Then he hit her. Had he connected he would have crushed her cheek-bone. As it was, his fist caught her high up, a glancing blow, and the ring cut a line along her scalp under her hair. She fell backwards and collapsed against the wall.

She was dizzy and for a moment had double vision. When it cleared, she found herself looking up at his trousered legs. He touched her with the point of a highly-polished leather shoe and said, "You want more?" He was dabbing at his cheek with a handkerchief.

"No," she whispered.

"Where's Susie?"

Even then her brain was producing alternatives. "She's with a friend."

"What friend?"

"He owns a hotel back along the Cape in Wellfleet."

"Okay, on your feet. You're coming with me."

"She may not be there. They were going shopping." She stood up, painfully.

"You're bleeding. Better get a towel." There was no sympathy in his voice.

She cleaned up her cut and he stood in the bathroom door, watching. It was not deep, but the hair had matted into it. She managed to free that, and stop the bleeding.

"Call your friend. Make sure Susie will be there," he said.

She picked up the phone and dialled the Fisherman's Arms. There was a click as the answering machine switched on. "This is the Fisherman's Arms. At the tone, please leave your name and number and the management will get back to you as soon as possible."

"David!" she screamed. "Walter's come. Take Susie to . . ."

She felt herself travelling backwards and landed in a heap

on one of the divans. Walter was holding the telephone. "You're playing games," he said.

He put the receiver to his ear. "This is the Fisherman's Arms . . ."

He slammed it down. "Wellfleet, huh? Okay, you've had your fun. I passed the Fisherman's Arms on my way here. I'm going there now. If Susie's not there, I'm going to the police." He hurried out.

She ran to the door and saw him behind the wheel of a red Buick, pulling away from the kerb. Then, surprisingly in this quiet area where few cars disturbed the peace, she heard a second engine, a screeching of tyres on tarmac and another car shot past the Buick. In the darkness, she could not identify it, could only make out dark shadows in the front seat. Even more surprising, Walter seemed to take off in pursuit and she saw two sets of flaring tail-lights racing away from her, towards Route Six. She did not wait to wonder why, nor who might be in the first car. She ran out into the street. The cold stung her eyes, making them water. She pulled her coat on, found a woollen hat in her pocket and dragged it down over her ears. In the other pocket were scarf and gloves, and as she ran she put them on, too. She went down Main Street, passed the little Post Office Square, turned right along a lane that led to the steps up the hill. Soon she was standing outside Pate's house. It was in darkness. She rang the bell and heard it echo through the house. She pushed again and kept her finger on it, every second expecting the door to open. But no one came. She bent down and looked through the letter flap as she had on the previous occasion. The door was not quite closed, for her pressure on the flap caused it to swing gently open. She was not yet conscious of apprehension, her entire concentration was on her need to get Susie away from Walter. Doors were left open for a multitude of reasons, often lights were turned off. Susie might be watching television. Pate might have taken her out for her banana split. She stepped into the hall. "Dennis!" she called. There was no reply. "Susie!"

She moved from the hall into the big living-room and switched on the lights. Everything was as she remembered it. "Dennis!"

She went into the suite on the right: bedroom, dressing-room, bathroom, neat and clean. Then into the other suite. It was the same. But something was wrong. An atmosphere. And then she had it. There was no evidence of anyone *living* in the house. Everything was in its place as might be expected in accommodation for rent, but there was nothing personal. There were no tooth-brushes in the bathroom, no slippers in the bedrooms. She pulled open hanging cupboards, opened drawers. All were empty. She ran back into the living-room and then she saw what she had missed the first time. Half hidden by a cushion on one of the big sofas was one of Susie's mittens. She picked it up. In that second, she knew that something was horrendously wrong.

She was in the street outside again, running. Steps. Lanes. Her eyes were streaming with tears. She found herself at the Fisherman's Arms. She banged on the door, but it was locked. She ran round the side and came into the restaurant through the doors which led from the beach.

The lights were not on yet, but there was a glow from the kitchen area.

"David!" she screamed.

The door opened and Peter stood there in his white tunic.

"Have you seen Susie?"

"There was a guy looking for you. Big, with a grey overcoat."

"*Have you seen Susie?*"

"No. Is there something wrong?"

"Where's David?"

"Christ knows. Look, can I help?"

"Susie's disappeared."

"Jesus! How?"

She was already turning towards the door. Hysteria was very close to the surface. "I don't know! Dennis Pate took her for an ice-cream. I went to the house to fetch her. They've gone."

"Gone?"

"Gone! With Susie! Oh, God . . . "

Sobbing now, she ran out of the door on to the beach, stumbling through the sand.

She reached the cottage and flung open the door, praying that she would see Susie and Dennis sitting at the coffee-table, waiting for her. But everything was as she had left it: the coffee-cup that Walter had been drinking from; a chair, knocked over during their struggle, lying on its side; the towel with her blood on it.

"Susie!" she shouted, but the only answer was silence.

In the middle of that silence, like some clamouring alarm, the telephone rang.

10

She picked up the receiver. "Yes?"

"Good evening again, Jane. This is Dennis."

Relief flooded through her body like a narcotic. "Dennis! Oh, thank God! Where's Susie?"

"That's rather what I wanted to talk to you about."

"I went to the house. It was in darkness, your clothes were gone. I didn't know what to think. Where are you?"

"Well . . . things have been moving along, my dear."

"Is Susie still with you? Is she all right?"

"Perfectly."

"Where is she?" It was like a cry across the great abyss.

"Jane dear, I want you to do a little something for me." For the first time, she realised how much she disliked his light voice, the meaningless endearments that punctuated his conversation."

"What's happened? Where's Susie?"

"We're never going to get anywhere if you keep on shouting."

"Is she hurt?"

"Of course she isn't hurt."

"Why haven't you brought her back?"

"If you stop being hysterical for a moment, we'll sort all these things out to our mutual satisfaction."

Every nerve-ending in her body was raw. She swallowed and tried to take a grip on herself. She was in the middle of a nightmare, and everything was out of control.

"Please," Pate pleaded. "For your sake and Susie's sake. For all our sakes, calm down."

"You said you wanted me to do something? What?"

"Now, that's better! First, before we continue our little chat, I want you to put down the phone, go outside and open the trunk of your car. Look inside, come back and tell me what you've found. Then we'll talk some more."

"Oh, no! Dennis . . . " Could he be sending her to find Susie's body?

He read her thoughts. "Don't be silly! How could you imagine such a thing?"

She collected herself. "Please . . . "

"Do it!" The voice was harder.

She stumbled from the house. The small white car was parked in the street. She opened the trunk and saw a black flight bag, with brass zips and several bulging pockets. In the present context, even this ordinary item, standing squat and ugly, was filled with menace. But certainly it was too small to contain even a child's body. She opened the main compartment. Newspaper had been folded into the top and she took it out. Under it were a dozen swollen, heavy-duty plastic bags, each filled with white powder. She began to tremble as she stood in the bitter cold, staring at them. Then she replaced the newspaper and closed the compartment. The smaller pockets also contained plastic sausages. She zipped up the bag, closed the trunk and went back into the cottage.

"I've done what you said." Her voice came out as a whisper and she had to clear her throat.

"Splendid!" Pate said. "So now you understand what we're talking about. It seemed sensible to show you, otherwise you might have thought we were playing games."

"Is it heroin?"

"Well, let me put it this way, dear, it's not talcum powder."

"What has this got to do with Susie? Or me?"

"We are having what might be described as distribution problems. And we are, alas, having to leave Margate."

"We?"

"My associates and I. For one reason or another, which I needn't burden you with, one of our little ventures has become—how shall I put it?—somewhat tricky."

"You don't write books," she said, dully. "And your friend, Fischer, isn't a painter. I already suspected that."

"Perceptive of you. Let's just say we have other interests as well."

"You deal in drugs."

"We are businessmen, my dear. Supply and demand, you know?"

"Did you kill the man on the beach?"

"Not I, personally," Pate said fastidiously. "I abhor violence. But it is as well that you realise what my colleagues are capable of, for it will lend a certain urgency to what we require you to do."

Her mind was still on Willis. She stood with the telephone pressed to her ear, seeing the body moving in the waves, remembering he had been working for Walter.

"But *why*? He wasn't a policeman. He didn't know anything about drugs. He—he came here for another reason entirely."

"No organisation is perfect. Things were beginning to go wrong. We suspected a spy in our midst. A stranger arrived, asked questions. What other reason had he for hanging around? So we made a mistake. Why, we even thought *you* might be the spy at first."

"Me?"

"You turn up out of the blue, claiming to be on vacation. Here? Out of season? I mean, you can't blame us, can you?"

"I want my daughter!"

"Of course you do, and you shall have her. Eventually."

She tried a plea: "You're English. So am I. Doesn't that . . . ?"

"I beg of you not to appeal to my sense of patriotism. A childhood spent below stairs in a house where one's mother is a servant does not equip one for anything but self-interest."

"I want to speak to Susie."

"Do you think that is wise?"

"I want to hear her voice."

"You're worrying yourself about nothing, my dear."

144

"I want to speak to her!"

"If you insist."

She heard voices in the background, as though a door had opened, and a rushing sound that might have been waves breaking on a beach.

"Mummy?" The voice was faint and far away.

"Susie!"

"I'm watching TV with Mr. Pate and Miss Blackstock . . . " she was cut off in mid-sentence.

"There," Pate said. "You spoke to her. I hope you're satisfied that all is well. I assure you she is being looked after like the little princess she is."

"What do you want me to do?"

"It's very simple. First, you'll need to pack some overnight clothes. If anyone should ask you where you're going, you're taking a trip to New Bedford. You're interested in the old whaling ports. You will go, instead, to Plymouth. A room has been reserved for you at the Harbour Motel, down on the port. This is your check point. The motel will be watched. We will telephone you there at midnight, precisely, to give you your next instructions. Please be there, Jane, for Susie's sake."

"Yes."

"Have you any questions?"

"How can I be sure that you will let Susie go?"

"Our problem has been to get the merchandise off the Cape. There's only one bridge open at the moment over the Cape Cod Canal. You may have noticed that the other is undergoing repairs. Unfortunately, we have discovered that the police are watching the bridge, so we cannot move the consignment ourselves. You can. When it is off the Cape, we will have no further need of you, or Susie. We will arrange the exchange for you tonight." His voice had lost the pedantic, old-world tones he had affected. Now he was cooler, more precise. "Would you like me to repeat the instructions?"

"I can remember them."

145

"One more thing: please don't thing it crass of me to labour this point, but should you go to the police, or to anyone else, for that matter . . . do I have to state the obvious?"

"No."

"Then this is not good-bye, but simply *au revoir*."

She had hardly put the receiver down and was sitting, gripped by a feeling of total helplessness, when the telephone rang again.

She picked it up, but could not speak.

"Jane?" It was David.

"Yes."

"Is something wrong?"

"No. Why?"

"You sound—is someone with you?"

"No."

"I'm not going to be able to see you this evening. Something's come up. I'll call you tomorrow."

"All right."

The telephone line was like an umbilical cord, holding them together. She could not bring herself to cut the connection, yet there was nothing she could say to him.

"Where are you?" It was all she could think of.

"Boston."

"What have you been doing?"

"Look, I have to go . . . "

"David . . . "

"Yes?"

Just then there was a loud knock at the street door.

"Jane?"

"There's someone at the door." She cupped her hand over the mouth-piece and called: "Who is it?"

"Mrs. Hemming. Ma'am, would you open up, please? It's the police."

She put the telephone down, cutting off David's voice, and began to move softly towards the door that led on to the beach. But suddenly the street door opened and Ellis stood in the entrance.

146

"Mrs. Hemming, the Chief wants to see you."

"What about?"

"He'll tell you."

"Can't it wait until tomorrow? I have to fetch my daughter."

"It can't wait." He was a plump young man with brown, curly hair and long eyelashes. His expression was determined.

"Will it take long?"

"Can't say, ma'am."

She thought of the flight bag in her car. She thought of Susie. As barter for one, she had to have the other. Nothing could be allowed to get in the way of that. She checked her watch. It was 5.50 pm. She reckoned it would take her two hours to reach Plymouth. She had until midnight.

She sat beside Ellis in the cruiser. Neither talked. She tried to control her tumbling thoughts, because she knew she needed to be calm. She must not give anything away. Why *did* Boyd want to see her? Had he found out something? Had Walter been to him? Would Walter be there now, waiting for her?

The car stopped and they went into Boyd's office. Jane braced herself to meet Walter, but the room was empty. Ellis motioned her to one of the chairs near the desk. He settled in one behind her. Again, they sat in silence. She stared at the short-case clock on the wall.

Six o'clock arrived. Then six-ten.

At six-twenty, she said, "I can't wait any longer. I must fetch my daughter."

"You tell me where she's at, ma'am, and I'll fetch her for you," Ellis said.

She realised her mistake. "No, thanks. She's nervous of strangers. I expect she'll be all right for a little while longer."

They lapsed back into silence.

The clock struck the half-hour.

At six thirty-five, Boyd came in, alone.

"Evening, Mrs. Hemming. It's a cold one. A cup of coffee?" She shook her head. "You won't say no, Chuck?"

Ellis grinned. "Why don't you go and get yourself one?"

No mention of Walter. No sign of Walter. The young policeman went through the door that led into the house. Boyd turned to his desk and opened a file. Jane recognised her signature on the single sheet he drew out.

"I'd like to go over your statement again, Mrs. Hemming."

"Couldn't we do it tomorrow morning? I have to . . . "

"No, we couldn't do it tomorrow. You are Mrs. Jane Hemming, right?" He had given an emphasis to her surname.

"You know that's right."

"Thirty-four years old. English. In Margate on vacation. Flying home in a few days' time."

They went through her movements since her arrival, and where she was staying. Jane watched the clock's big hands move slowly round the dial, watched the pendulum track backwards and forwards.

They reached her description of the picnic: how she and David and Susie had lunched by the fire, how Susie had collected pebbles and then come back to them. He took her through every word, reading slowly and precisely. They had tucked Susie up in a rug and she had fallen asleep.

"What happened then?" Boyd asked.

"We sat around the fire and finished the wine."

He tapped the statement and said, "It says here you thought you saw a log at the water-line and you went to look at it and it wasn't a log, but the body of the deceased, Harry Willis. You sure about those movements?"

"Of course I'm sure."

"I went to the beach by Shoal Point light this morning. I found your fire and sat down where you sat and I have to tell you that from there you couldn't have seen the body. You couldn't see the water-line, even. You were sitting in a hollow."

She stared at him, taken aback. "We—we didn't see it exactly from where we were sitting," she said hesitantly.

'Uh-huh.''

"While Susie was asleep Mr. Maclean and I went up to look at the ruined house in the dunes."

The Chief folded his big square hands on his lap. "You didn't tell me that before."

"I didn't think it was important."

"Mrs. Hemming, that's what everyone says. When they leave something out, they say they didn't think it was important. You just tell me everything and I'll judge what's important. So . . . you went up to the old Moorhead place with Mr. Maclean. To look at it. And later, you claim, you saw some guy there, watching you."

"Yes."

"Anything else?"

"What else could there be?"

"You asking *me* that, Mrs. Hemming?"

She frowned. "I'm not sure what you mean."

"You know what I mean, all right. But let me spell it out. Maclean takes you for a picnic to a lonely beach. No one else around, except your little girl. She goes to sleep and he says, come up and look at the Moorhead place. You think you're the first woman to be taken to 'look over' the Moorhead place?"

She watched him, saying nothing. A slight flush spread over his cheeks. "I know that house," he went on. "They're always doing it in there. Never mind it's dangerous. It's dark and private. Men with girls half your age. Men with men. We're a gay community in summer."

"Do you enjoy this kind of talk?" she said.

She saw that she had angered him. Then he said flatly, "Tell me your version of what happened."

"You've already made up your mind."

"I want to hear you tell it."

"We went to look at the house, that's all. And Mr. Maclean told me the story about the old man from Boston who lived alone there until he died. We were on the verandah when we saw the body, only we didn't know then what it was."

149

"Oh-kay." He pronounced the word in two distinct parts. "We'll leave it at that for now, but we'll come back to it. So you were standing on the verandah . . ."

"The storm was about to break and we were talking about getting home. Then David . . . Mr. Maclean, saw what he thought was a log and said he'd race me to it before we left."

"So you ran down and found it was a body."

"And he went to call you while Susie and I sheltered in the house."

'Right.'' He put the single sheet of paper back into the folder and took out several others which were stapled together. They were photocopies and there was an official insignia at the top of each page.

"And neither you nor Mr. Maclean knew the deceased?"

"That's right."

"Well, now, there's a funny thing," he said thoughtfully. "I told you it was my job to find out why Harry Willis had come to Margate. Seems he was hired by a man named Hemming." He glanced at one of the sheets. "Mr. Walter Hemming." He leant back. In spite of the room's warmth, she felt cold.

"Would you like to comment on that?"

"I told you I didn't know the man."

"Coincidental. I mean, here's a lady with a small child comes to Margate at the beginning of winter and her name is Hemming. And here's a PI from New York been hired by a man called Hemming who fetches up here, too."

"It's not an uncommon name."

"I looked in the Boston directory. There aren't too many Hemmings. But leave that aside. In police work you don't buy coincidence, no matter how small. Now this Mr. Walter Hemming: what do you know about him?"

Was he trying to trap her? Was Walter here, listening in another room? If he was, nothing she could say would make any difference. If not, maybe there was still a chance she could bluff it out. Fight! she thought. Deny everything. If Boyd thought she did it, make him prove it.

"Nothing," she said.

"You know I'm going to check this?" She remained silent. "Now look . . . " His voice changed. " . . . why don't we save ourselves a lot of trouble? I mean, listen, do you think that if you admit knowing him I'm going to say straight out you killed him? It's not like that at all. This is what I think happened: I think you left your husband. You had an argument, a fight, something like that, happens all the time. Then you took the kid and ran. How does that sound so far?"

She did not reply.

"Okay, so what does your husband do? He knows you're going back to England, he tries to find you before you leave. He hires a PI called Harry Willis, who tracks you down and then . . . well, we have to work out what happened then, but he ends up dead, that's for sure. Now all we got to do is find this Mr. Walter Hemming, link you with him, and the DA's got a case. See what I mean? You help us now and you're going to do yourself a lot of good; you hold out and make us work our asses off and no one's going to be helpful to you. What do you say?"

"I say I've never heard of Mr. Hemming and I know nothing about a New York private detective and I'm going back to England in a few days. If you have any more questions, I want to talk to the British consul in Boston, if there is one, or our Embassy in Washington."

She saw his eyelids drop as he calculated the trouble in which that would involve him.

He tucked the photocopies back into the folder. "Well, you had your chance. I wouldn't bet on that England trip." He slapped the folder shut. "If you didn't have a kid I'd put you away till we got some answers, but I'm not that kind of a bastard. I'm going to get Ellis to drive you back, but you better not put a foot out of that cottage tonight. I want to know where you are every minute while I make a few more inquiries."

"I'll walk back."

151

"You do what you want, just remember what I said. We'll be watching you."

The cottage was only three blocks away, but she was frozen by the time she reached it. The cold was brutal; she had never experienced anything like it. As she pushed the door open she saw the police cruiser. It came slowly along the street with Ellis at the wheel. He raised his hand as he passed, but she did not acknowledge it. She let herself in, locked the door behind her, went to one of the street windows and peered through the blinds. The car's tail-lights were disappearing up the street, then it made a U-turn and came slowly past the cottage again.

She tried to clear her mind of the panic which hovered on its periphery. The problem of delivering Pate's bag had become much more complex. It was no longer a matter of simply driving into Plymouth, she had first to get out of Margate without being observed. She could not use her own white Ford, that was certain. She must find another car. David had a car, but he would have taken it to Boston. Then she remembered Peter Davidson's old Chrysler. Should she ask him if she could borrow it? But she would have to make some explanation. Why not just take it? She could always say . . . she tried to think of an excuse. Then a voice inside her skull shouted: never mind excuses! Take the car.

She looked at her watch and as she did so, she heard the police cruiser pass the house again. It was now nearly seven-thirty. She had four and a half hours to reach Plymouth. Plenty of time.

She stood by the window, watching the cruiser's movements. They were repetitive: having passed the cottage after its U-turn, it turned right past the Fisherman's Arms towards the centre of town. Ten minutes later it nosed its way back, repeating the process.

She hurried into the bedroom and packed, flinging Susie's belongings and then her own into the smaller of her two suit-cases, until it was full. She had no intention of returning to Margate. When she had delivered the flight bag and Susie had been returned, she would drive straight to Boston airport and take the first available plane out to New York, Washington, Dallas—anywhere. And then home. The clothes she could not fit into the case, she left hanging in the closet. Anyone coming into the cottage to look for her and seeing them would not immediately assume she had left town.

After making sure that the cruiser was out of sight, she ran to her own car and brought the flight bag inside. She had not picked it up before and she was surprised how heavy it was. She had no idea of the value of the heroin it contained, but she had read about small amounts being worth millions on the street. This was no small amount.

A few minutes later, the police car made its way past the cottage again, turned and slowly drifted back into the town. She gave it a couple of minutes, then, carrying the flight bag and her own suit-case, went out of the door on to the beach and towards the hotel.

The bags were heavy and she moved through the sand with some effort. The Fisherman's Arms loomed up ahead, the lights in the restaurant on. She left the beach and went round the far side of the hotel to its small parking lot. Davidson's Chrysler was parked next to his dune-buggy; there were no other cars. She opened the door of the Chrysler and put the suitcase and the flight bag on the front passenger seat. She slid in and pulled the door closed as softly as she could. The key was in the ignition. She held her breath, turned it, and after a few misfires, the engine caught.

At that moment the rear door of the restaurant opened and she saw Davidson's square, heavy figure silhouetted against the light. He was bringing out some empty cardboard boxes for incineration.

"Hey!" he shouted.

She put the car into gear and thrust her foot down on the gas. The back wheels spun on the gravel, the car fish-tailed across the lot and out on to the street. As she fought for control, Davidson shouted again and began to run towards the dune-buggy.

153

She did not know whether he had recognised her or not. She turned away from the beach, into the town's smaller streets. Her inclination was to get away as fast as she could, but she realised that this would only attract attention, so she drove sedately. As she halted at a cross-street she heard the open exhaust of the dune-buggy. Ahead of her was a short drive-way which led into an open, private garage. Without hesitating, she drove into it and cut the lights and motor. She heard the throb of the dune-buggy come closer, and watched it pass, running smoothly on its over-sized wheels. She gave it a minute, backed out of the garage, drove towards the beach and picked up the beginning of Route Six. When she reached the town limits she put her foot down.

The road passed through the dunes and they looked like mountains of spun sugar in the brilliant moonlight. Everything was still, frozen. At any other time she would have been stunned by its bleak beauty, but now all she could think of was reaching Plymouth. She did not allow herself to anticipate that anything might go wrong with herself or the car, or that Pate would not call her at midnight. And just below the surface of her mind was the recurring problem of Walter? Where was he? Why had he disappeared so suddenly? Getting Susie back was her immediate objective, but after that she would still have him to deal with.

She drove watching the road and alternately the rear mirror, and it was not until she was a few miles short of Orleans that she saw the lights behind her. They were faint at first, winking and blinking like moonlight on water. Then, slowly, they began to gain on her. She put her foot down until it was on the boards. The old Chrysler wheezed and rattled. The speedometer needle reached its limit between sixty and seventy. Still the lights crept up behind her.

She told herself that other people used the road at night: ordinary people; people going about their innocent business. But she felt in her bones that these lights, as far as she was concerned, were not innocent. What would she have done had her car been stolen. She would have gone to the police.

The lights drew nearer until they were not more than fifty yards behind her. The road fell away in a long downhill slope. The Chrysler gathered speed. As it dipped, the car behind her was visible against the moonlit sky. She could see its strange superstructure: it was the dune-buggy.

At any other time, she would have been relieved that it was not the police, but this was not any other time. Davidson was just as much a threat now as anyone else.

She saw a side road going off to the right and swung the car on to it. She found herself driving through a community of holiday houses, all closed up for the winter. Dirt roads cut away from her on either side. She began to twist and turn. The moonlight was bright enough to drive by and she put out her lights. She drove on dirt, then on tar, and back on dirt until finally she could no longer see the dune-buggy's lights.

She came to a bigger road. There was a glow in the night sky away to her left which indicated this was Orleans. The road seemed to lead her in a circle round the town. She took it, hoping it would bring her onto the Mid-Cape Highway.

She drove for mile after mile. The dark road closed in like a tunnel ahead of her. Gaunt and leafless trees reared up on either side, their branches stark against the sky. A breeze had sprung up, which made the air even colder. The landscape was alternately silver and black as clouds passed over the moon. She drove deeper into a wilderness of sea marsh and dunes until she lost all sense of direction. The road narrowed, there were no sign-posts. She had left her maps in the cottage. She told herself she must stop and ask the way, but she had not passed a house for a mile or more. The country flattened out and she could see a long distance across fields, or what she thought were fields, but there were no lights.

She pulled over and stopped. She must have gone wrong, missed a sign in the dark which would have pointed her to the Highway. For all she knew, she might be circling towards Margate. She decided to go back and check.

As she was turning the car, she saw in the headlights that what she had thought were fields were, in fact, sheets of water, lying in huge flat pans. Of course! These were cran-berry bogs. She had been here before. And the water was not water, but ice, looking like burnished steel.

All she had to do was follow the road down a few hundred yards further and she would come to the line of beach houses at East Sandwich, the point where she and Susie and David had turned back to Margate. *Where Susie had seen the brown car.* The brown car. The car which belonged to Willi Fischer. And Willi Fischer, sharing Pate's house, had to be another member of the drug-smuggling group. He would almost certainly have been in on Susie's kidnapping.

Her thoughts began to race. The men would have needed a place to hold the child while Pate made his arrangements with Jane. Might not that place be here in one of the closed beach houses? Who would come here in winter? A few bird-watchers, people collecting driftwood. It was a perfect hide-out and, since Fischer's car had been here, he was familiar with the area. Suddenly, she experienced a powerful feeling of Susie's presence, that she *was* here, within a few hundred yards.

With renewed hope, she backed the car into an area of bush where she was sure it could not be seen from the road. It was not until she was moving towards the row of houses that she began to wonder what she could do if she did find the child. She could not go blasting into the house like a television hero. She realised that she did not even have a weapon. She should have looked in the car for a spanner. But she had never hit anyone in her life.

The cold made her gasp. Here by the sea it was less dry, and the damp cut into her. She began to shiver.

The moon was bright, but she kept to stands of scrub pine and melted into their shadows, pausing every few moments to look and listen. The whole place was as silent as the grave.

The road forked left and soon she saw a low line of dunes against the sky. The beach houses were built along the tops of the dunes so that they rose and fell like waves. On her left, behind a heavy hedge of brush, lay the frozen cranberry bogs;

ahead of her, the cottages. She came through the pines and stood, looking at the road. It was empty. There was no brown car. There was no car at all.

What if Susie had been wrong? What was it she had said: the thin man? Susie talked of so many men. Red. Blue. Thin. Fat. But Fischer was the thin man. And she had been right about the blue man. Perhaps they had already left the area and taken Susie with them. Perhaps her own deductions were wrong. Perhaps they had never brought the child here.

She felt the blown sand crunch under her shoes. The place was desolate in the frozen moonlight. Each house had a little path leading to the road, each was separated from its neighbour by about ten feet, each faced the sea and had a deck on front. In summer they would have been cheerful, if not luxurious; now they were ominous, dark, brooding places, their windows boarded up, old gas bottles lying outside, broken fencing, smashed paving—the detritus of summer. They stretched away in the darkness; a dead colony in a dead landscape.

Then she heard the noise. It had sounded—was it her imagination?—like a voice. She stood, holding her breath, hearing the surf and her own heart beating. It came again: half-heard. It might have been a cat, a wild animal. She moved on, near the houses now, using their shadows as she had used the shadows of the trees. She flitted like a dark ghost from one back porch to another, stopping, listening, looking into the dark areas.

Two houses along from her, something glittered. It caught the edge of her sight as the moonlight struck it. She stopped, thinking it might be a dustbin, or something left over by a summer visitor. She moved closer. A cloud passed over the moon and she lost the reflection for a moment. Then it came again. It was the rounded end of a car bumper. There was a car-port between two shacks and the car had been driven into it. In the dark, she could not tell what colour it was.

She crept forward and more of the car became visible. She then noticed a faint crack of light showing through the boarded window of the house beyond the car. She stood still for nearly a minute, making certain that there was no one in the car itself. She went forward again, using the car as cover, until she was flat against the wall of the house.

She could hear voices now, not separate words, just a rumble of speech. She put her eye to the crack, but all she could make out was the corner of a table and vague shapes moving between the light and herself.

If Susie was in the house she might be in the bedroom. From the shape of the cottage she thought that this was a living-room, perhaps with kitchen combined. She began to work her way round the far side. She found another window, also boarded, but there was no light beyond it. She had now investigated both sides and the rear. It only remained for her to go to the front. This would be the most exposed part. But if she wanted to see who was in the main room, there was no other way.

At that moment, a door opened. It must have been warped like the cottage doors in Margate, for she heard it scrape on the floor. She ran back the way she had come, taking cover under the porch of the next-door house. She heard steps on the concrete path that led round the house and then she heard the door of the car open and close. She waited for the engine to start, but nothing happened. She edged forward so she could see into the car-port. The person in the car had a flashlight. The beam flickered low down, then it turned upwards, illuminating his face. It was David.

She could not believe it. It was not possible. In her shock, she moved backwards without taking enough care and stumbled into a dustbin. Immediately, the light was killed. The car door opened again. She turned and ran along the side of the house. Another beam, this one more powerful, moved over the walls of the houses. She stumbled on. Someone shouted. There were confused yells from behind her. For a few moments, only instinct directed her movements, for one thought had taken over her mind: David *was* her enemy. Her early suspicions had been right. All his understanding and sympathy, his concern and warmth, had been contrived to keep her from suspecting the truth.

She knew that she must not be caught, must not be identified. If they found her here, they would never let Susie go.

She ducked between two houses and ran on to the beach, but this was a mistake, for the sand was heavy and huge groynes made of boulders had been built out into the water to break the force of the waves. She clambered over one, sliding and slithering, bruising herself, and behind her the pursuit gathered momentum. She heard more shouting, then, incredibly, the crack of a gun and the shining ricochet of a bullet from a boulder ten yards away to her left. Her panic gave way to terror.

She threw herself down the far side of the groyne and raced back towards the cottages. She tried the door of one, but the owners knew all about vandals and it was securely locked.

Beyond the road she saw the glint of ice on the cranberry bog. Her car was on the other side of it. She started to dash across the road and there was renewed shouting as someone heard her. Pine trees lined the bogs, but sparsely, and she knew they would not give her any cover. She saw a light away to her left. They had cut off her road to the car. There was only one way open: across the bog.

She put out her foot to test the ice. It felt solid. She went down on her hands and knees and began to crawl, feeling the cold strike up through her clothes.

Twenty yards away, a voice shouted: "Over here! Over here!" She dropped flat on her stomach. The moon was bright, illuminating the ice like a floodlight.

Below her, she saw Walter.

His face was only inches away from hers, his mouth frozen into a rictus grin.

She felt a scream rise in her throat and stuffed a gloved hand between her teeth. She choked and gasped, unable to take her eyes off the thing encased in the ice. He lay on his back, arms spread out, eyes open, staring straight at her.

There was a great, crescent-shaped cut in his throat, a second mouth, from which the edges had peeled back like lips.

She could not move. Her pursuers were all around. She felt the bile rise as it had when she had seen the body on the beach. She must not vomit. She closed her eyes, but the face remained on the emulsion of her mind, as it always would remain.

How long she lay there she never knew, for she went into a kind of limbo. When she came to her senses, she heard the voices of her hunters growing fainter, and then, after a few moments, the sound of car engines. They were taking Susie away. She had lost her chance. Slowly she began to crawl from the monstrosity below her, too dazed even to wonder how it had got there. She moved along the edge of the bog and pulled herself up the bank on the far side like some primeval water-creature seeking land. Five minutes later she found her car.

She sat in the driver's seat, clammy with cold and horror, and when she looked at her watch she saw that she had less than two hours to get to Plymouth. But which way to go? She tried to recall something of the journey with David and Susie, anything that might orientate her in this black, featureless landscape, but everything was muddled in her mind. She knew that if she turned right, it would bring her to East Sandwich again, so she must go left. After driving for less than a mile, she came to a junction where three roads met. There was something familiar about it, and she realised it was the point at which David had lost da Souza. She went straight on and soon she saw a light ahead. It seemed to come from a house—no, not a house: something bigger; a building standing by itself in a small clearing among the trees. Shutters covered the downstairs windows, but fingers of light came through them. Then she saw, near the top of it, a sign. It was not illuminated, but in the moonlight, she could read it. In letters a foot high it said: UNCLE'S.

She stopped the car at the roadside. Someone were would

surely be able to tell her the way to the Mid-Cape Highway. The door was locked. She banged it with her fist. After a few moments she heard footsteps and the door opened. She stepped in, seeing the bar, the booths, the video game that Susie had played. The man who had opened the door was standing with his back to the light and she could not make out his face.

"I'm trying to get to the Mid-Cape Highway, but I think I'm lost," she said. "Could you . . . ?"

The door closed and a voice said softly, "Hi, teach! You come to give me that lesson?"

She looked into the dark, broad face of Julio. He had stepped between her and the door.

Feeling trapped, she repeated: "The Mid-Cape Highway. I wonder if you could tell me . . . "

" 'I wonder if' . . . I got to remember that. 'I wonder if you could tell me.' That's terrific. That's real English. I wonder if you want a little drink? Is that right?"

"Not now. I'm in a hurry. Some other time, perhaps."

He took her arm and she felt the strength of his fingers. "I love it! 'Perhaps.' You drink wine, perhaps?" She felt herself being moved towards the bar. His body was close to hers and as he leant towards her she smelt his breath on her cheek. Suddenly, she was transported back into the ruined house on the dunes, with the storm raging and the rancid, winey smell and the man, standing . . . It had been Julio's smell!

There was a two-litre bottle of red wine and a half-filled tumbler on the bar top. He splashed more wine into it and held it out so she was forced to take it.

"Cheerio," he said. "That's English. Pip-pip." He had already been drinking from the glass. For a second she thought of throwing the wine into his face and making a run for it, but the thought died, still-born.

"All right, one drink," she said. She put it to her lips, trying not to shudder.

"You like it?"

"Very nice."

Play it cool. Don't annoy him. Edge towards the door.

"Very nice," he mimicked. He took the glass, drank, refilled it and pushed it in front of her. "You know, I was beginning to wonder what I was going to do tonight." He put a hand on her shoulder, gripping it. She tried to twist away. His other hand slid inside her coat, moving on her body.

"You're a terrific looker," he said. It was the phrase Walter had used.

"Please!"

"Please? Is that English for you want some?"

"No. It's English for stop."

"Please is stop?" He was rubbing her breasts.

"For God's sake!" she said, pulling away.

He turned, pressing her against the bar, his thighs against her. "You like to dance?"

"No."

"I don't mean all this new shit. I mean the old style. You know, bodies together. If you want, I can put on the juke box."

Without warning, he pulled her coat back over her shoulders, trapping her hands and arms. His knee was forcing her legs open and his hands were busy at the front of her bra.

She fought. She struggled and bit and kicked. He put his mouth on hers and forced her teeth open. She tasted his saliva and she wanted to vomit. She felt as though she was falling, but she knew that if she fell, she was done. She heard her own name. How could he be calling her name? His mouth was imprisoning hers. Yet the name rang in her ears.

Abruptly, she was released. Julio stumbled backwards and she saw Peter Davidson behind him. He had his arm locked around the other man's throat. Davidson was shouting: "Jane! Are you okay?"

Julio was powerful. He knew how to fight. He caught Davidson by the hair and beard and began to pull him forward over his shoulder. It was brutal. They fell on each other, grinding and tearing, hitting, butting. Bar stools broke, a booth was smashed. Jane ran. She bolted from the room, across the dark driveway and, in a matter of seconds, was racing away up the road, scarcely registering that Davidson's dune-buggy had been parked beside the Chrysler.

Ten minutes later she saw a sign saying "Sagamore Bridge" and she knew she was on the right road at last. She glanced at her watch. Time was running short.

She had almost reached the bridge when she recalled Pate's words: "We have discovered that the police are watching the Bridge . . . " And she was carrying the heroin. In her concentration on Susie she had almost forgotten the threat to herself if it should be found. She slowed to a sedate thirty-five miles an hour, resisting the voice in her mind which was repeating insistently: "Hurry! You must *hurry*!"

She drove on to the bridge, seeing only the dark roadway stretching ahead of her. There was little traffic. New Bedford, she thought . . . English tourist . . . no, if she were stopped by the police she would say she was a writer, researching the history of whaling . . .

And then, while she was still rehearsing, the Bridge was behind her and she was on the road to Plymouth.

She put her foot down and reached the Harbour Motel at 11.52. She was sitting, hunched in a chair in her room when, precisely at midnight, the telephone rang.

"Good evening, dear." It was Pate's voice. "Have you brought the bag?"

"Yes." It lay at her feet. She could not remember having brought it from the car.

"You *have* done well."

"Where's Susie?"

"She is perfectly safe. Don't you worry about her."

"What is she doing?"

"What do you think a little girl would be doing at this time of night? She is fast asleep."

"I want to talk to her."

"I'm afraid that will not be possible."

"Please!"

"You'll be seeing her soon enough. I'm not going to wake

her now." His voice was brisk, the tone final. "Now for your instructions. Are you ready?"

"Yes."

"Tomorrow morning at ten o'clock you are to take Route 3A West and you'll come to the Plimoth Plantation. Have you heard of it?"

"It's the re-creation of the original colonists' village."

"Precisely. Now listen carefully. You are to park in the main lot. Go into the museum first. Then to the theatre where they show a movie about the Plantation's origins. Watch it. We'll be making sure no one has followed you. Walk down the slope into the village itself. It is surrounded by a high stockade. You'll find it is a single street with houses on either side. There will certainly be bus-loads of school-children and other visitors walking around. Become one of them. Behave as you would if you were an ordinary tourist. Do you understand?"

"Yes."

"Go into each of the houses on the left side of the street. Chat with the villagers, if you like. Don't hurry. Visit the garden of the third house. It is hidden from the street. When you have made sure you are alone, leave the bag under an old, wooden wheelbarrow you will see there. Continue your tour. When you reach the end of the street, work your way back on the opposite side, again going into each house. If everything is clear, Susie will find you."

Before she had a chance to speak, he had hung up and the line went dead.

In spite of the heat of the room, she was cold when she got into bed, and felt sick with worry and betrayal. So David had been one of them all along. He had cultivated her and made a play for her, for one reason only: he wanted to use her. He might even have killed the New York detective or, if he had not killed him, he had certainly been party to it.

A dope-runner. It explained his sudden absences; it explained everything that had puzzled her. She had eventually believed in him because she had wanted to believe, but all the time he had been watching her, stimulating this reaction, encouraging that reflex, conditioning her for the time when they would decide to use her, getting to know her well enough to predict accurately her responses when her child was threatened.

She lay in the big bed, trying to control the shivering that had racked her intermittently since she had seen the horror in the ice. Had David also murdered Walter? Poor Walter; he'd had to contend with the violence in his own make-up, but could never have imagined that his own end would be so savage. Somehow, he must have got in their way and they had simply eliminated him as they had eliminated Harry Willis.

By comparison with her discovery of his body, the set-to with Julio belonged to another world; it was a world she hated, but could understand. She could never understand the cold-blooded indifference to life which led to calculated murder.

She wondered what had happened at Uncle's after she had run, but she did not wonder for long. Her mind was filled with the fear of what might happen to Susie.

She wanted to cry, but she no longer seemed to have the capacity; she was drained, dried up. There was not even the luxury of anger, for she must not allow anger to distort her judgement during the coming day. She must stay cool, in command of herself. Forget about David. Forget about Walter. For the moment, think only of Susie. She must dismiss any suspicion that they might not keep their side of the bargain. Do everything as she had been told. No mistakes. No lapses. And then perhaps—God, no! She mustn't think like that. She *would* get Susie back.

She wanted to sleep so that unconsciousness would bridge the time until morning, but had to lie for hours, staring into the dark, until exhaustion came to her aid.

11

When she awoke it was already light. For the first few
moments she lay in a warm ball, hovering between
wakefulness and sleep, her mind a blank. Then she opened
her eyes and the first things she saw were the black flight bag
and Susie's mitten on the chair. Everything came rushing
back, filling the room with nightmare. And with this came
panic, the fear that she had overslept. She looked at her
watch: eight o'clock. Reassurance. Two hours before she was
due to leave for the Plantation.

From her window she looked out over the harbour. The
day was grey, the sea calm, but there were few people moving
and those who were wore heavy parkas and hats with flaps
over their ears. Deserted at this hour, *Mayflower II* swung at
her moorings.

She had not eaten since lunch the day before. It felt a
lifetime away. She knew she should have something, if only
to stop herself from feeling faint. She washed her face and
put a comb through her hair, not even bothering to look in
the mirror. She wondered whether she should take the flight
bag with her, and was tempted to put it under the bed and
come back for it. But a cleaner could find it and, possibly,
open it. She took it.

She walked up Water Street and found a Mug'n'Muffin
bar where she ordered coffee and toast. She drank the coffee,
but could not swallow more than a mouthful of the toast.
Even that lay on her stomach like a lump of unbaked dough.
It was nine o'clock when she asked for the bill. Still time to
kill.

She went out into the street again. The thermometer above

Woolworth was reading nineteen degrees Fahrenheit. Wondering if she was already being watched by Pate or Fischer or even David, she wrapped her coat tightly around her, pulled her woolly hat down and covered her mouth with her scarf. She slung the flight bag over her shoulder and walked back to the motel.

As she drew near its parking area she saw something that had not been there before. A glimpse of it over the hedge was enough: it was the flashing light on top of a police car. She had almost reached the parking lot's entrance and was afraid she might attract attention if she turned and doubled back. So she went on, walking steadily. There were two policemen standing between their own cruiser and the yellow Chrysler. At some point last night Davidson must have reported the theft.

She walked on around the motel to the harbour. She could not go back to pay her bill now and would have to leave her suit-case. Fortunately, she had her passport, credit cards and travellers' cheques in her purse. But she was leaving a trail behind her. She remembered how David had told her she had as good as drawn a map for Walter's investigator when she had left New York. She was doing the same again, and sooner or later they would catch up with her. If it was later, she did not care. She would have Susie and they could do as they liked. She would help them. At the very least, she could identify Pate, Fischer, da Souza and David. She could give details to the police of everything that had happened, chapter and verse, she thought viciously. Margate, which had seemed at first such a happy refuge, had turned out to be a place of horror.

She walked about half a mile along the sea-front, past the restaurant where she and Susie had had lunch and where, for the first time, she had felt safe from Walter. Now she was safe from Walter forever, but the thought gave her little comfort.

She could not go back to the car, so she would have to take a taxi to the Plantation. But wouldn't the police be watching

167

for that? They could have broadcast her description. Taxi-drivers had radios. With CB, everyone these days seemed to have a kind of universal, mobile communication. Then she saw the little bus that had so delighted Susie. "Plimoth Plantation Transport Company" was lettered on its side and it drew up at a stop a few yards ahead of her. She ran towards it.

"You going to the village, lady?" the driver called.

"Yes!"

"Climb in."

There were several tourists already in the bus. It turned up on to Main Street and then took the coast road out of Plymouth. In a few minutes it turned off, ran along a country road for a mile or so and stopped at a large car park that was almost empty, apart from a string of bright orange school buses. A party of children shepherded by two teachers was passing through the gate into the village and from the noise on the far side of the fence she realised there must be many more already inside.

She paid her admission and the woman in the booth said something to her. Through the children's chatter, Jane could not hear what it was. The woman repeated it and seemed to make a gesture towards the flight bag. Jane remembered how, in an IRA-tormented Britain, most art galleries and museums now insisted that all visitors' bags must be searched for explosives.

"What?" Her voice was stupid with fright. Such a search was something for which even Pate had not bargained.

For the third time the woman said: "The combination, honey! Do you want the combination ticket for the village and the *Mayflower*?"

"No." Relief flooded through her. "We—I've been to the *Mayflower*."

"That's a real pity. It's cheaper with the combination."

Jane tried to smile. "I'll remember next time."

"Sure. You from England?"

"Yes."

168

"My mother came from England. A town called Winchester. Know it?"

"I know it well."

"I was there once. It's *so* beautiful."

A line had formed. The woman handed Jane her ticket. "You're going to enjoy this," she assured her.

"Thank you."

"My pleasure. Have a good day now."

The friendly exchange had steadied her nerves and she took time to check back over her instructions. Pate had said she was to go to the museum first, then watch a film. Behave as though she was an ordinary visitor. How did ordinary visitors behave? She could hardly remember. Trying to relax the lines of strain on her face, she walked on.

She pretended to look interested in the photographs and exhibits in the museum, but she was seeing nothing. She had to wait for a few minutes outside the little theatre before it emptied of schoolchildren who had been at the previous showing. They came out, laughing and kidding around. Some were not much older than Susie. She stared at them with longing.

She tried to lose herself in a group of adults who all seemed to be carrying shoulder bags, some like hers, some larger, some smaller. She sat in the centre row of seats, with elderly women on either side of her. The short presentation consisted of slides with a commentary, showing how the local historical society had built the village as an exact replica of the original of 1627. She could not remember any of its details afterwards. When it ended, she came out and prepared to follow the final set of instructions.

The Plantation's setting made her think of a movie set, built for an early fifties Western. She was faced by a high wooden palisade into which a large gateway was set. Over it was a wooden construction called The Fort, from which the early colonists had defended the village against the Wampanoag Indians. She went through the gate and the village lay ahead of her, on sloping ground. There were little houses on each side of the dusty street. Some were tiled, but others were thatched, one-room log cabins. Each had a tiny plot of land behind it for gardens and animal pens, with runs for hens and geese.

The street was filled with children in bright parkas, their noses pink from the cold, running and shouting, darting in and out of the houses, followed by harassed teachers. Here and there she saw members of the Plantation staff playing their roles as members of that first group of colonists.

The men were dressed in knee-breeches, coats of dark serge, light waistcoats and shirts with wide, falling collars. Most wore large black floppy hats and many were heavily bearded. The women, on this bitter day, wore long dark cloaks that fell to the ground, and white cotton caps.

Jane hesitated, confused by the very nature of the place, with its mixture of the contemporary and the historical. Then her eyes began to search the mobs of children in the hope of seeing Susie. But they would never let her become visible now. She would be kept hidden until the last possible moment. Be natural, she told herself. They'll be watching. Do what they said. Go into the first house.

It was crowded and she could see almost nothing. She pretended to look at the old agricultural implements on the walls, then she emerged and walked the few yards to the second house.

There were five or six children with a teacher in this one. The floor was of packed earth and there were no windows. The place was dark, dusty and smelled of smoke. A Pilgrim Father was tending a fire over which a cooking pot had been hung.

"Do you have fires like this in England?" one of the little girls asked. There was the same look in her eyes that Jane had seen in Susie's on the *Mayflower*, total belief that the man *was* a British colonist of 1627.

He simply nodded and went on with what he was doing.

"What are you cooking?" she said.

"Food," the Pilgrim Father said shortly.

170

"She means, what sort of food?" the teacher explained.

He ignored her and went on with his task.

"Well!" she said indignantly, "you might at least try, when they're interested."

He paid no attention.

He did not look up until the children had been taken out, then he glanced around at Jane. For a moment, she thought he was going to speak to her, but he turned back to the fire. He had a sparse grey beard and his clothes were dusty with wood ash. Deciding she had spent enough time to appear natural, she followed the children out.

At the third house, desperately trying to remember her instructions accurately, she took a path round the side to the plot at the back. There were beds of summer vegetables, blackened now by the frost, and maize cobs hanging up to dry. A pig of some breed unfamiliar to her was penned behind wooden hurdles. Then she saw the wheelbarrow. It was old and broken and had a solid wooden wheel. It had been turned upside down.

She looked about her, but the visitors seemed to have decided that it was not a day for examining gardens—even the pig appeared to be cold—and most of them were crowding into the houses, where there were fires. She placed the flight bag on the ground next to the wheelbarrow, as though she were resting for a minute, and pushed it out of sight with her foot. Then, pretending interest, she inspected the dead vegetables before moving slowly on towards the next house. She completed the row and started up the other side, always looking for a small girl with large brown eyes and straight, shining hair, wearing an orange parka.

She realised how perfect a place the village was for a change-over. Susie would simply be one of a hundred kids. No one would even notice her. In her imagination, Jane could already hear her cry: "Mummy! I'm here!" as she had heard it in the court-room in New York.

In each house, she waited for a few minutes, then went on to the next. One was empty. She stood alone and shivering in

171

the cold, pretending to look at seventeenth-century artefacts, not daring to deviate from her orders.

In the next house a woman in costume was kneading bread. She was younger than most of the others and was wearing traces of make-up, an anachronism Jane imagined was not permitted the quasi-Pilgrims. She seemed indifferent to the children who came in and out, only half-listening to their questions, giving the briefest possible replies.

A child asked: "How long do you have to bake the bread?"

"A long time," she said vaguely.

"How long?"

"Four or five hours."

"My mother bakes bread," the child said. "It doesn't take that long."

"I bet she's got an electric oven."

"Sure."

"This one's wood."

Jane went on. But no little girl materialised at her side. She wondered whether they would send Susie to her as part of a group or let her loose by herself.

She finished her tour of the houses and decided to start again in case she had been moving too quickly. She wanted to run, but told herself, *be natural*. She went in and out of one cabin after another. She saw a dozen children of Susie's height in orange parkas. She hurried up to each in turn and peered into their faces. Then she began to criss-cross the street, visiting houses at random, although she knew this was not what Pate had ordered, that she was no longer acting naturally. But the movement of visitors was such that people hardly seemed to notice her.

As time passed and she walked and she waited in one house or another, she had to face the growing conviction that she had been a fool ever to let herself believe that they could be trusted. But what else could she have done? If she had not agreed to Pate's terms, her last hope of getting her child back unharmed would have gone.

At first she tried to tell herself that she must be wrong. She had carried out her orders precisely. They *had* to produce Susie.

But after what seemed an age of searching, shivering in the bitter cold, she knew it was hopeless. Pate—and David—had been too clever. They had known she could identify them and must have decided to hold Susie until they were safely out of the country. Would they release her even then, or simply dispose of her? Standing at the end of the Plantation's unsurfaced street, looking despairingly at the rough-hewn log cabins, the "Pilgrims", the tourists, she suffered a moment of such desolation that she had to fight the temptation to approach some total stranger and pour out her story.

Then a thought came to her. Perhaps the bag had not yet been collected. They would probably have waited and watched to make sure she had come alone. If she were to take it back, she would still have something with which to bargain, would put them in a position where they would have to trust *her* for a change.

She hurried to the garden. The bag was still in place. Oblivious of passers-by, she ran towards it. As she bent to pick it up, a movement caught her eye. A man, carrying an identical bag, was disappearing between two of the houses. Many visitors were carrying bags, as she had already noticed, but there was something familiar about the man. She lifted the bag from under the barrow and realised it was lighter than it had been. She unzipped it and saw that it was empty. Either they had taken the drugs or it was a substitute, an attempt to keep her from discovering too quickly that the original one was gone.

She ran into the street, searching for the man she had seen, intending to cut him off. But he was already near the main entrance.

"Stop!" she called.

He half turned. It was Willi Fischer.

"Stop!" she shouted again.

He began to run.

173

Tourists, alarmed, were turning to stare at her. Someone grabbed her. She swung round and hit out with her free hand. It was Dennis Pate, huge in his black overcoat, the Beatles' cap pulled down over his face.

"Stop that!" he snarled. "You'll never see Susie again!"

But she could not stop. She struck at him again and he hit her with the back of his hand. A Pilgrim Father suddenly appeared about ten feet in front of her. She recognised him as the grey-bearded man in the dusty coat who had irritated the school-teacher. Now he was holding a gun in his hand, not a seventeenth-century muzzle-loader, but a modern, blue-black pistol. It was pointing directly at her.

It was only then she realised how thoroughly she had been duped. They had watched her every step of the way. They had known her movements. This man was one of them, one of Susie's kidnappers.

As these thoughts flashed through her mind, she saw the gun come up. He was going to kill her now, as they must already have killed Susie. Pate jerked her sideways. She fell to her knees. She heard the sound of the gun and felt its pressure wave. She heard a woman screaming. Then the grip on her arm dropped away. She looked around. Pate was falling. He seemed to take forever. As he fell she saw the blood on his coat, the gun in his hand.

The grey-bearded Pilgrim ran forward. Behind him was a woman in a dark cloak—it was the young one, who had inadequately removed her make-up—and another man holding Willi Fischer against the stockade fence. The man had taken possession of the flight bag. He, too, held a gun.

All the strength seemed to leave Jane's muscles and she slipped into a sitting position. There was a ringing in her head and her sight became blurred. She fell on to her side, legs bent under her, fists clenched. The dusty man, who had shot Pate, sank on to his haunches at her side. "Mrs. Hemming, are you all right?" he said.

"Where's Susie?" she said. "Where's my daughter?"

Another colonist emerged from a house. He was holding a

174

rifle and a walkie-talkie. Others were clearing visitors from the village. She had no idea what was happening. All she knew was that there was no Susie and that she must not give in to the dizziness that was threatening to overwhelm her. She was aware, away to her right, of someone running. There were shouts, and then, for one brief moment, she saw David. He was high up on the stockade platform called The Fort. He, too, had a gun in his hand.

"There!" she cried, pointing towards him. "There he is!"

As she tried to struggle to her feet, he fired. She heard a cry. Then he disappeared. She heard another shot, then another. But now everything was slipping away from her, and the world went dark.

She opened her eyes and looked up into Maclean's face. She put up her hands to ward him off. She thought: this is a nightmare. He took her hands and held them. She tried to free them, tried to beat at him.

"Jane, it's all right! You're safe."

She was lying on a rickety wooden bed. As her eyes grew used to the gloom, she saw that she was in one of the Pilgrims' houses. She could smell the old wood smoke and the damp, dirty floor. She was so cold she was shaking. Beyond David she saw one of the colonists and the woman in the long cloak.

"You okay, Mrs. Hemming?" the colonist said. He was pulling off tufts of his beard with his fingers.

"Who are you?"

From an inner pocket he pulled out a leather flap case and held it open. She saw a badge and, behind a plastic cover, a photograph and some writing.

"I thought . . . " she began.

David released her hands and she put them over her face. "I thought you were . . . "

"We've got most of them," the dusty man said. That's what Susie would have called him: the dusty man.

"Where's Susie?"

175

They looked down at her. No one spoke.

"Is she . . . ? Tell me! If she's dead, don't keep it from me."

"We don't know," David said. "That's the honest truth. We don't know."

For the first time, she cried. She still had her hands to her face and she fought the tears, pressing her fingers against her eyeballs until they hurt. But the tears squeezed under her fingers and down her cheeks. She turned away, and they let her cry.

After a few moments, she heard movement and when she was able to look, she saw that the policeman and the policewoman who had been dressed as colonists had left, and only David remained.

"What now?" she said.

"Now I take you back to the motel."

"What are you going to do?"

"We still haven't got them all. There are road-blocks all over the Cape and on every road out of Plymouth."

"You don't know whether Susie is alive or dead?"

"No, I don't."

"So what are you going to do?" she repeated.

"I'm going to East Sandwich. Going through every one of those shacks. We'll take the whole Cape apart."

"I want to be there."

He shook his head.

"Why not? I'm her mother!" ("I'm her father, goddam it," Walter had said. Now the father was dead and perhaps the child was dead, too.) "You can't stop me. If you don't take me, I'll come anyway."

Less than thirty minutes later they were driving along the Inner Cape. At first she sat in silence and he did not interrupt it. Then, as they crossed the Sagamore Bridge he said: "This is where we picked up your trail last night."

"So you knew all about it, and you didn't try . . . " There was anger and bitterness in her voice.

"It's not what you think. It wasn't cut and dried like that."

"You decided to *use* me! And Susie!"

"Only at the Plantation when we were there to protect you. And never Susie. Christ, what do you think I am!"

"I don't know."

"We have time to talk. Let's take it from the beginning . . ."

As they drove, he talked, and she listened, because listening occupied the surface of her mind and diluted her aching fear for Susie. Slowly, a picture of the last week emerged, much as she had known it, yet not exactly. The facts were a tangle of threads criss-crossing each other. If you picked the right thread and pulled, everything came undone, but if you picked the wrong one, it drew the threads into a knot.

She realised that from the moment she had arrived in Margate she had, in a sense, lost control over her actions, unwittingly becoming part of a scenario she did not even know was being played out.

For David, it had begun as far back at 1968—which had seen the beginning of her own adult story, too.

"Remember Flower Power and Haight Ashbury?" he said. "And 'Make Love, not War?' Well, the other side of that coin was that at the same time more heroin was reaching the streets of America than at any other time in history. Drug-taking reached epidemic proportions. Washington had to do something to counteract it, and do it fast. So the Government set up the Federal Bureau of Narcotics and Dangerous Drugs under the authority of the Attorney General, bringing together agents of the former Bureau of Narcotics and of the Dangerous Drugs Department of the Department of Agriculture. Remember a movie called 'The French Connection?' "

She nodded. "Then you'll know that at that time, and from even before World War II the major heroin output was from laboratories in and around Marseilles. It was decided that the only way to stop the drugs reaching America was to attack their source. So Washington began to put heavy pressure on the French Government. I'd joined the Bureau after my wife was killed and was one of the agents sent to work with the French Office of the Prevention of Drug Traffic in Paris.

"After eight years, we believed we had checked the manufacture of heroin and morphine in the South of France and Corsica. But trying to stop the drugs traffic is like trying to pick all the mushrooms in a field. When you think you've found them all, the next day brings a new crop.

"The manufacturers went to ground for a year or so, then started up again with opium brought in from Turkey, Iran and the Golden Triangle.

"A couple of years ago I was working with a partner in France and London when we had a call from a woman who said she had information about a new operation involving the United States.

"She wouldn't come to my office—I was working in Marseilles as the time—and for a while we couldn't agree where to meet. She didn't want to be seen with me and I didn't want to be led into a trap, identified and . . . well, removed by interested parties.

"Eventually we met one winter's day at Senequier's on the port at St. Tropez. I remember it was sunny and we sat outside, looking at the yachts and drinking hot chocolate.

"She was a good-looking, elegant woman, but she was an addict and had become a courier for one of the European drug rings some years before. She had served time in Belgium and France for drug offences. But now she had become infatuated with a man much younger than herself. She knew that if she was arrested a third time she'd spend years in prison. End of romance. She wanted to make a deal: she'd continue her work as a courier for the ring—it was the only way she could make enough money to support her habit—but in return for a guarantee from us that she would not be arrested, she would turn informer and tell us all she could about the ring's movements."

"You'd make a deal with a woman like that?" Jane said.

"We needed her more than she needed us. We came to

an—arrangement. Then she told me about a new operation. She didn't know much, but she believed that consignments of drugs were going to be run from Le Havre to somewhere in the Caribbean and from there to the United States. It took us eight months to trace the exact route: from Le Havre to Martinique, and then by private yacht up the East Coast of America. Somewhere along the coast they were transferred to other boats and taken ashore.

"At first we were convinced they were coming ashore on Long Island, but then we had a tip-off that more heroin than usual was reaching the Boston streets, so we shifted our operations further north."

For weeks, he said, they had no success, but then an abandoned yacht was found by the Coastguard thirty miles north-east of Provincetown. It had been badly damaged by fire, but surviving papers gave its home port as Martinique. As soon as David had heard about it, he'd had the yacht brought to Boston, where it had been taken apart, plank by plank. When traces of heroin had been found, he had decided to concentrate his efforts on Cape Cod.

"I'd known Bill Dugan at college," he said. "He wanted to sell the Fisherman's Arms, so we decided to buy it and use it as cover. There were four of us working together. Kaminsky—he was the guy in the false beard at the Plantation—worked out of Hyannis, and I had two others on the Cape.

"At first everything appeared to be normal and we thought we'd made a mistake. There was no evidence of anything out of the ordinary."

"What about Pate and Fischer? They were unusual, surely. Weren't you suspicious when they arrived?"

"They were already here, and *they* were suspicious of me and had inquiries made. Fortunately, my cover stood up, largely thanks to Dugan, who assured them I was a lawyer who'd had a breakdown and had been advised to find less demanding work. It was when he reported the inquiries that I knew I was on the right track, though at first I didn't get on to Pate and Fischer. Of course I wondered about them. I was suspicious of everyone. Even of you, at first.''

''Me?''

He shrugged. ''In this business, you find yourself wondering about your own mother.''

''But surely, to someone like you, they were obvious? Even I realised they weren't what they pretended to be.''

''Everything's obvious in hindsight. At the beginning, they didn't put a foot wrong. They appeared to be exactly what they seemed, two middle-aged gays playing at being artists. This place is full of them in summer and autumn. But because they *were* false notes, I watched them, especially when they didn't migrate south with the rest of the summer people as the weather changed. Then I began to notice other incongruities . . . ''

''Like their friendship with da Souza? He was such an improbable friend for them to have.''

''Sure. Again in hindsight. But it took me a while to spot it, because I'd actually introduced him to them in the bar one night. Christ, they must have laughed up their sleeves at that!''

''I wondered about you in your role as bird-watcher,'' she said. ''Always on the dunes. Always looking out to sea. Were you watching da Souza's boats?''

He nodded. ''I realised his were the only ones they could possibly use: fishing-boats free to come and go at any time of the day or night. I watched them for days, and finally I found out how they were running the stuff once they got it ashore: deep-frozen under the cod and haddock in the refrigerated truck.''

''So that's why da Souza was so angry with Susie when she ran towards the truck the first day we were here.''

''He must have wondered if she'd seen anything. The problem was that there was no hard evidence to connect Pate, Fischer and da Souza. I mean, in the business sense. And then there was Julio, who owned the truck. Remember him?''

''Yes, I remember him,'' she said grimly.

"We decided to pressure them, try to force them into the open. A few weeks ago we let them see more police around the place, we began to set up road-blocks, so they would start to wonder if we were on to them. And they did exactly that. The stuff piled up in Margate because they were too scared to run it. But their distributors in Boston were calling for it, so the pressure was coming from both sides.

"How did you know all this?"

"We had an informer—I'll get to that later. Anyhow, something had to happen—and it did. You arrived. Right smack in the middle of it all. You were a complication I didn't need."

"But you wanted me to stay! After I'd told you about Walter, I remember Dr. Maclean prescribing—what was it? Rest, relaxation, good food. With him."

"I wanted to have you under my eye while I had your story checked." He paused. "There were—other reasons, too."

"I understand how people like you are suspicious of their own mothers. So you thought I was another of them, come to help out?"

"Why not? You were at least as suspicious a character as Pate and Fischer, arriving out of the blue at the beginning of winter. So I bugged your phone and—" He held up a hand to check her outburst. "Be glad I did! That's how I heard your conversation with Pate. That's how we were able to listen in to his second call and hear the details of the Plantation hand-over. I wanted to stop you right then, but I was over-ruled. It was too good a chance to pick them all up. I did try to warn you, though. I went to the motel this morning, but you weren't there."

"You went . . . ? Were you in a police car?"

He nodded. "It was a risk, but I reckoned that by then Pate and his friends would already be at the Plantation."

"I saw the police car. I thought they were looking for me because I'd stolen Peter Davidson's car. I took the bus to the Plantation."

"Was that it? It didn't matter. There was no turning back

at that stage, for you or us. I just wanted you to know you weren't alone.''

She thought of something: "You searched my cottage, didn't you?''

"How did you know?''

"You knocked the Saki out of position. Did you try the door at two o'clock one morning, after you had left your note about the picnic?''

"No," he said sharply. "You didn't tell me about that. It was almost certainly Willis, maybe hoping for a chance to snatch Susie.''

She shivered. "When did you finally believe I wasn't working with them?''

"When Willis was identified.''

That was the one part of the whole episode she already understood. And once she knew about the drugs she had even understood why he'd had to die.

"Who killed him?''

"I don't know yet. Da Souza and Fischer are dead. Pate's unconscious. I would guess it was da Souza.''

She leant back and closed her eyes. David's story, the unravelling of the loose ends, had briefly taken her mind off Susie. As they sped along the empty roads she thrust the nightmare away again, forcing herself to talk, to ask questions.

"Pate was suspicious of me, too. He said he thought someone had been spying on him.''

"He was right. Someone had. Do you remember the European woman I told you about? The one who'd tipped me off?''

"Did he know her?''

"Not at first. She came up from New York to join them not long before you arrived. She was my informant. You saw us together one day.''

"You mean . . . ?''

"Stephanie Hirsch.''

"I thought you and she were . . . ''

182

"Yes, I know you did. And no, we weren't."

At any other time, she might have been pleased by that. Now it made no difference.

"You want to talk about what happened next?" he said.

"I know what happened next. They took Susie. And your Stephanie Hirsch doesn't seem to have told you about that."

He frowned. "We've been out of contact for more than twenty-four hours. But I think it must have been a spontaneous decision by Pate. Probably he saw a way to get you to move the stuff and he grabbed Susie on the spur of the moment."

"And took her to that house at East Sandwich."

"What makes you say that?"

"I guessed. Like you did."

"How did you know I'd . . . ?"

"I saw you there." She told him about the night before, how she had seen him illuminated by the torch, how she had found Walter's body.

"My God, that I didn't know about," he said. "And we thought you were one of *them*. How the hell would Walter have got there?"

She described Walter's arrival at the cottage and how he had left to go to the Fisherman's Arms. More slowly, thinking it out, she said: "I heard two cars. He must have reached the door just as Pate was driving past, seen Susie in the car, and followed."

"He probably thought Pate was helping you. He must have chased them down to East Sandwich and then, thinking he was one of us, they killed him and dumped his body."

Grateful for his deliberate avoidance of sympathy, she said: "But Susie wasn't at East Sandwich."

"No. At least, not when we arrived. We went through it thoroughly. I think they only used it for brief meetings—a place where no-one would be likely to see them all together."

"I'm sure Susie *had* been there. I could—I could *feel* her."

"She probably had. It was the logical place for them to have taken her. I think Walter's arrival upset their plans—

they suddenly realised that it wasn't a safe house any longer. For all they knew, we had it under surveillance and they couldn't risk staying. So they took her somewhere else. I would guess, not far away.''

''Where? And what about Stephanie Hirsch? Can't you get in touch with her? She must know.''

''I've tried. I hoped she'd call, but there's been no contact and I don't know where she is. She wouldn't have gone along with a kidnapping, I'm sure of that.''

''She went along with murder.''

He shook his head. ''I find that difficult to believe, too. There must be some reason she hasn't been able to call.''

They turned off the Highway, following the signs to East Sandwich.

''Do you really think . . . ?''

''She'll be there, Jane, somewhere in those shacks. There's no place else they could have moved her.''

The road wound through the cranberry bogs, still frozen in the dull winter light. They turned a bend and passed a building on their right.

''David! Stop!''

He slammed his foot on the brake and the car slithered on the road surface.

''It's Uncle's,'' she said, pointing.

''What about it?''

''Maybe—maybe Susie . . . ''

''Why should she be there?''

''We met Julio there, remember? And, David, I'm sure he was the man in the ruined house. I noticed his smell then, and again last night.''

''Could be,'' he said, thoughtfully. ''They probably took it in turns to keep an eye on you. They were as suspicious as I was—of everyone.'' He paused. ''What do you mean, again last night?''

She told him quickly about her encounter with Julio.

''I . . . wonder. It would be almost as good a hide-out as the beach-house. It's only open for lunch and very few people come here.'' He swung the car off the road and left it in a stand of pines. ''Let me check. You stay here.''

''I'm coming with you.''

The place looked more menacing in daylight than it had at night, with its peeling paint, its faded signs, its loose boards. It had the rickety, abandoned air of all lonely buildings, shuttered and silent. There were no cars in the parking-lot, no evidence of any living person.

As he looked at it, David said: ''Julio's the only one left. He could be there, waiting for them . . . ''

''With Susie.''

''And if she's there, Stephanie might be with her.''

He went on to the wooden verandah and tried the door. It opened and they went into the dim bar. Now, in the aftermath of the fight between Davidson and Julio, of which she had clearly seen only the beginning, it looked very different from the first time she had seen it. One of the booths was splintered, bar stools lay on their sides. The wine bottle from which Julio had been drinking lay on the floor and a pool of red wine had spread over the floor-boards.

''Wait here,'' David said. ''I'm going to check the rest of it.''

There were several rooms beyond the bar and she could see into the kitchen. Gun in hand, David went in.

It was cold. Everything was still. Then, alone in the silence, she thought she heard a sound. To her right was a wooden staircase leading to the top floor. The sound, a kind of whimpering, seemed to come from above. She ran across the room and began to climb the stairs, every sense straining. She found herself on an upstairs landing, with four doors leading off it. She heard the whimpering again, as she opened the first door. It was a bedroom. The shutters were closed and the room was in darkness. The sound came again. ''Susie?'' she said. But there was no answer.

She switched on the light. In the centre of the floor was the source of the whimpering: Peter Davidson. He lay on his side. His face looked as though it were made of lumps of raw

185

steak. Both his eyes were closed and blood had spread from his broken mouth and dried in a crust on his cheek. He was unconscious, but he was alive.

She went back into the corridor, but before she could call David, something touched her hand, like a raindrop. It was sticky, almost black. Blood.

She looked up at the ceiling and saw there was a closed loft entrance above her. Stains showed at the edges of the trapdoor where dark droplets had gathered.

The hook for the loft ladder was against the wall. She pulled down the trapdoor and the ladder came with it. She went up, sick with dread at what she might find.

The loft had a dormer window and the winter light streamed in. It was full of junk: a broken bed, old gas heaters, stained mattresses, lengths of copper tubing, battered basket chairs.

Someone was sitting in one of the chairs.

Jane screamed. It was a scream to freeze the blood, like human fingernails scraping down a blackboard.

The thing in the chair was Stephanie Hirsch. She had been stabbed over her left breast, several times. The blood had run down her body and formed a pool on the ceiling boards, like the pool of red wine in the bar.

Jane stood, frozen, and could not turn away even when she heard David's feet on the ladder. He pushed her aside and went towards the chair. She heard him say, "Oh, Christ!"

Now she knew there was no hope. Now it was just a question of where in the house she would find the small, dead body. She was standing in the dormer window and she turned blindly towards it, her back to the room.

The window overlooked the rear of the building, with thick scrub and trees behind it. As her eyes focussed, she saw something alien amid the harsh midwinter greys and blacks and browns. A flash of yellow. She stared at it and the focus became more precise. It was Susie's scarf. It hung, like a little flag, on one of the dead branches of a bush.

"David! Look!" Her voice was soft, almost unbelieving.

"What?"

"It's Susie's scarf. It's Miss Blackstock!"

He saw it, then he said sharply: "What's that?"

"Where?"

"Past the scarf."

In the tracery and patterns of the winter trees and bushes there was a darker shadow, square, monolithic.

"It's a truck," she said.

He slid down the ladder, hardly touching the rungs. She followed.

They ran out of the front door and round the side of the restaurant and as they did so she heard the noise of a big diesel starting up. She followed David down a track that had been cut into the brush.

"Wait!" she called. But he was already twenty yards ahead of her.

Then, making straight towards him, she saw the Mack truck which had been parked on the jetty in Margate. Julio was at the wheel.

"David!" she screamed, but he stayed where he was, crouched in the middle of the track as the vehicle raced on, a great, living thing, shaking and vibrating like an elephant in its death charge.

Then she watched his arms come up, almost in slow motion, one supporting the other. She saw Julio's face in the window of the truck. She heard the whiplash of a shot and saw the windscreen craze over. David fired again. Glass splintered where she had last seen Julio's head.

The truck lurched to the left, its weight ripping through the brush. It hit a tree, glanced off, hit another and then, with a tearing noise, it came to rest against the side of the building.

David wrenched open the driver's door. For a moment, nothing happened then, very slowly, Julio toppled out. There was no mark on him, but his head was at an acute angle to his shoulders.

David reached into the cab and switched off the engine. Then he ran to the back of the truck and opened the big double doors. The only thing inside was a pile of old fish boxes and sacks.

He swung himself up and began to pull the pile apart. Then she heard his sharp intake of breath and a call: "Jane!"

Sick with apprehension, she clambered in beside him and went down on her knees. Susie lay among the sacks, her lips moving in fluttering, bubbling sighs. She was sound asleep.

David picked her up and examined her quickly, as Jane waited, hands clenched by her sides. Susie's cheeks were flushed.

After a moment, he smiled: "She's all right," he said. "I suspect they gave her something to make her sleep, but she's okay. Here, you take her."

Jane held out her arms and took her child.

12

Jane and David were standing on the cottage's sun-deck, huddled in coats against the bitter cold. As she looked across the beach she thought that the jetty looked curiously deserted without the fishing-boats and truck she had become accustomed to seeing.

"What will happen now?" she said suddenly.

He shrugged. "Hard to predict, but I hope we've put an end to drug-running in this area for a while. Pate's the only one left alive."

"Have you talked to him?"

"He didn't regain consciousness until yesterday. I had a few minutes with him before I left Boston. He's talking his head off—being 'helpful', he calls it."

"So many people dead in a week," she said. "It's been one long nightmare."

He put an arm around her shoulders and she leant against him. "It's over now. You have to try and forget it, for Susie's sake as well as your own."

"I know. Fortunately, it's affected her less than I thought it would."

"She has Miss Blackstock," he said, smiling.

Jane had spent the morning at the little hospital where Susie had been kept under observation for the past forty-eight hours. She was recovering with remarkable speed and her memory of being kidnapped was almost nil because she had been kept in a drugged state. She was already something of a favourite among the nurses, who were bewildered by the number of people, ranging from a prince and a gentleman named Sir Henry, to Miss Blackstock, with whom she was on familiar terms.

Jane had hardly seen David, who had left for Boston soon after Susie had been delivered to the hospital, and had returned this morning.

"They let me in to see Peter while you were with Susie," he said.

"How is he?"

"All I could see were two slits staring out of the bandages, but he's going to be okay. He took a hell of a beating from Julio: two ribs cracked and his right wrist broken. He's lost teeth and both eyes were nearly closed."

"I feel dreadful about him," she said. "I involved him by taking his car. I wish I could do something for him."

"Don't worry. I'm going to see he's taken care of. The department has a fund for cases like his. Incidentally, da Souza owned Uncle's."

She stared at him. "How did you find that out?"

"Pate. He told me da Souza bought it a few months ago with his share of the money. Julio lived there."

"And—Stephanie?"

"Peter couldn't talk much, but he managed to tell me something about what happened. After the fight Julio dragged him upstairs and into the bedroom. He was only just conscious, but he saw Stephanie go past the door, carrying Susie. He thinks that she was trying to get away. The last thing he remembers before he passed out was Julio going after her."

"Do you know, of all the people I've met here, Peter was the only one who was exactly what he seemed," she said bitterly. "How long will he be in hospital?"

"At least another two weeks."

"He was like me, caught up in something he didn't even know about. David, where do *you* go from here?"

"That depends on a number of things. Right now, I go to eat. How about you? Hungry?"

"Ravenous."

"Sea-food?"

"Steak."

"I've never come across such a carnivorous woman. Here we do the best seafood in the whole of the United States and all you want is meat. Come on, then, I know a place on Main Street."

They talked idly during the meal, both carefully steering away from anything that might touch on events of the recent past.

It was not until they were having coffee that he said: "When do you leave?"

"I'm booked out of Boston the day after tomorrow, assuming Susie's all right."

"You won't change your mind and stay over?"

She shook her head. "I have to pick up my life. I want to get home and settle down with Susie and forget all this."

"I've been doing a lot of thinking these past couple of days," he said slowly. "After we get things cleaned up here, I've got nearly six months leave due. What I want more than anything is to pack a bag, pick up my fly-rod and take off. I used to fish in England and I want to fish all the old places again, and find some new ones. In Scotland and Ireland, perhaps. Do you like fishing?"

"I've never tried it."

"Shall I come and knock on your door, wherever you are, and give you the chance?"

"Are you serious?"

"Very much so. And when I've finished fishing, I'm going back into law. This game's getting too dangerous for cowards like me. You interested in respectable attorneys? Or are they a bit dull after what you're used to?"

"If someone told me, you're going to sit in a rocking chair by a fire in a village somewhere for the rest of your life, and the most exciting thing you'll ever see is the postman, I'd be very happy."

After he had paid their bill they walked out into the street. He took her arm.

"Do you remember what we talked about in the house on the dunes?" he said.

"Yes."

"You said something about being for it in principle, but not then. You said you would take a rain-check."

"I remember."

"Well, we've had the check. What about the rain?"

She looked up at the sky. "The clouds are gathering," she said.